Michael Sheehan (Mícheál Ó Síocháin) was born in Gorey, Co. Wexford in 1962 and grew up in Co. Cork. He has lived and worked in Barcelona, Laredo, Washington DC and London, and has now returned to his home in Co. Cork. He currently works as a lecturer in Limerick, and is married with three children.

Since 2010, Michael has had numerous short stories short- or long-listed for national awards including: Francis McManus Short Story Competition, William Trevor Award, Over the Edge New Writer of the Year competition, Penguin/RTE short story award, Hennessy New Irish Writing Short Story Competition, Carried in Waves Short Story Competition, Glimmer Train Short Story Competition and Mercier Press Fiction Competition. In 2017, he won the Over the Edge short story competition, as well as their New Writer of the Year 2017/8 award.

The Sugar Sugar Café is Michael's first novel.

First published in 2018 by Dalzell Press.

Dalzell Press
54 Abbey Street
Bangor, N. Ireland
BT20 4JB

ISBN 978-0-9563864-3-4

The Sugar Sugar Café

A Novel

Michael Sheehan

Dalzell Press

Dedicated to Noreen

Contents

Chapter 1:   The Sugar Sugar Café, 2012 (Player: Alice Woods)

Chapter 2:   Carl O'Shea, Chef, 2012 (Player: Carl O'Shea)

Chapter 3:   Pictures of Jesus, a story from the past (Player: Alice Woods)

Chapter 4:   Rain on a Tin Roof, a story from the past (Player: Carl O'Shea)

Chapter 5:   Brief Encounters, 2012 (Player: Burnt Toast)

Chapter 6:   Choosing My Confessions, 2012 (Player: Alice Woods)

Chapter 7:   Billy Frankenstein, 2012 (Player: Billy Woods)

Chapter 8:   The Auld Triangle, a story from the past (Player: Jerry Doyle)

Chapter 9:   Avenger, a story from the past (Player: Carl O'Shea)

Chapter 10:   The Last Days of The Pavilion, a story from the past (Player: Burnt Toast)

Chapter 11:   'Go For Tuna', 2012 (Player: Jerry Doyle)

Chapter 12:   The Electric Monkey, 2013 (Player: Alice Woods)

Chapter 13:   Shiane's First Communion, 2013 (Player: Carl O'Shea)

Chapter 14:   Yoghurt, 2013 (Player: Burnt Toast)

Players

Alice Woods: mother of Billy, native Buffalo girl and waitress at The Sugar Sugar Café, Rathluirc

Billy Woods: son of Alice and schoolboy at Rathluirc Christian Brothers School

Carl O'Shea: chef at The Sugar Sugar Café, and sailor

Jerry Doyle: owner of The Sugar Sugar Café, entrepreneur and lover of women

Burnt Toast: bookkeeper, blogger and amateur film reviewer

One

The Sugar Sugar Café

2012

Player: Alice Woods

The Sugar Sugar Café

Larry Gogan's on the radio, shooting the breeze about his early days as a pirate deejay, making it sound so cute. Larry's voice is like honey poured over Cap'n Crunch. The worn out buggy pushers and the yummy mummies are all done and gone, and it's too early for the brotherhood of Alcoholics Anonymous.

My only customer is a high school skipper who's trying to squeeze the pus out of a humongous zit. Just for the hell of it, I call out to him, 'Everything alright there, hon? Can I get you another coffee? A pair of pliers maybe?'

'Good Vibrations' comes bouncing out of the radio and I sway my hips in time. I watch Carl, the chef, pouring burnt oil from the deep fat fryers into empty milk cartons. He's wearing a dirty Smiths T-shirt, surfer shorts and sneakers. The slogan on the back of the T-shirt reads 'Meat is murder'. Carl scratches high above his knee revealing part of the Betty Boop tattoo on his left thigh. He claims he got his tats done in a bordello in Panama when he was in the merchant navy. Says he was drunk with a couple of mates on shore leave, got into a knife fight with some locals, got arrested and missed the boat out of Panama City.

Carl is five feet nothing—but he claims that in Panama he was a giant. He dumps the cartons of oil into the dumpster out in the alley.

'Any chance of a latte?' the school kid says in his cute Cork accent.

'Tole you already hon, we only got regular coffee here.'

'How's about a cappuccino so, like?' he says.

'Cappuccino's not regular, hon. Say, shouldn't you be in school today?'

'No.'

'Sure you should. Everybody's got school today.'

'Shouldn't you be in an American circus?' he says.

I wipe the ketchup stains off the laminated menu and look out the window at the traffic going by.

My son, Billy, was twelve years old yesterday. Twelve years old. I can hardly believe it. Billy has attention deficit hyperactivity disorder. The medical folks shorten those words to ADHD, but the abbreviation doesn't come close to describing the problems Billy has. There ought to be some kind of warning sign that tells you to raise your voice whenever you say those words. Those words ought to be written large like the Hollywood sign: ATTENTION DEFICIT HYPERACTIVITY DISORDER. Nothing can describe the temper tantrums, the screaming, the restlessness, or the crying. Nothing.

Simple things can set Billy off. We could be sitting at home watching TV and if the phone rings or the door buzzes, Billy can turn from this beautiful child into a possessed demon. When Mattie, his deadbeat dad, was around he used to call Billy his 'little shark', on account that Billy never stops moving.

Billy goes to St Stephen's School for Boys; it's a regular school but Billy's in fifth class when he ought to be in sixth. He's had his fair share of setbacks and he gets bullied sometimes. I blame his teachers; they just don't know how to handle him. Billy needs constant stimulus or he gets bored and that's when the trouble starts.

Sometimes Billy will ask a question or two in class and the teachers don't like it. They say no other boy asks so many questions. The teachers think there's badness in him. It's not badness; it's a chemical imbalance and that's what causes his spells. Just last month he got sent home from school for threatening to smash a teacher's head in with a pencil box. Hasn't everyone wanted to say that to a teacher at some time or other? He's a good kid, really he is, and talented too. When we're in the park, Billy can lay his head on the ground and hear the grass grow.

***

We were living in New York when Billy was diagnosed with ADHD. It wasn't any great surprise that he'd some sort of medical condition. At least we finally had a name for it. I've heard other moms say that their children never slept as babies, but in Billy's case it was true.

My mom would call me every other day from Buffalo offering advice. She used to say Billy needed more discipline; we needed to spank him more. When we spanked him, she called us unfit parents and threatened to call the cops. Next, she blamed it on too much TV; she said the damned child got all his learning from the TV.

Then she blamed the toons and the sodas and candy bars; and then it was all New York City's fault.

Mattie claimed he always understood that there was something not right with the child. He said I'd been in denial about the whole thing for years. When Billy threw himself out the bathroom window, dressed in his Superman suit, expecting to hover in the air like he was Clark Kent Jnr, we realised the problem was beyond us. Luckily for

Billy, we lived in a brownstone, only one floor up, and he landed in the bushes.

The doctors gave us medical leaflets and names of books to buy, and Billy was prescribed Ritalin. In the beginning, each time I'd give Billy his Ritalin meds, I used to say a little prayer that this would be the pill that finally cured him. Mattie and I thought it was going to be a temporary thing. Nobody told us it was going to last forever.

Billy felt special, seeing all the different doctors; there was a different one every time we called to the medical centre. Some doctors increased the dosage of meds; some decreased it. When they upped his meds, Billy lost weight but his moods stabilized. He was never a great eater but now he had no interest in food. The doctors told Mattie and me not to worry about his weight and to try taking Billy to Roy Rogers and McDonald's; if that's what it took to get food into him, then that's what it took. The doctors gave us phone numbers of various support groups around Manhattan and we stepped into this whole new world—the world of being the parents of an ADHD child. It was there we learned it would last forever.

The first thing you get to learn as the parents of an

ADHD child is that nobody loves your child. That's the very first lesson right there. People pretend they do, but they don't. Not the nurses, not the doctors—especially not the doctors—not the shrinks and not even your own family. You and your problem child are more than an inconvenience to everybody else. Your child is a freak and guess who you are? You're the parents of that freak.

It was in a cold parish hall on East Thirty-Seventh Street that we first listened to other parents of ADHD children tell their stories. They looked a lot like us: tired. Mattie held my hand as we listened to the stories. Most of the parents were having problems with their little boys. Not so many had problems with girls. Their stories sounded a lot like ours: the screaming, the fighting, the cost of meds, schoolteachers who didn't give a shit, schoolteachers who didn't even know what ADHD meant. Doctors who didn't give a shit, doctors who charged for prescription refills. Some parents had two and three children with ADHD. I couldn't imagine what their lives must have been like. I know God will forgive me when I say that if you have one ADHD child, why the fuck would you want another? When some of the parents started calling it a 'gift', I sighed and gripped Mattie's hand tighter. Lemme tell you, it's no gift.

Then one fine day, Mattie announced we were moving to his home place in Ireland. Just like that. Like he had solved a niggling clue in a crossword puzzle. Everything would be a whole lot better when we moved to Ireland. He never asked me if I wanted to go or even what I thought about the idea. As far as he was concerned there was no need for a discussion; the solution was so obvious. Mattie described the fresh air and the green fields and the education system that was second to none. And his parents, Bridie and Ollie, would love to help us cope with Billy. I was just too tired to put up an argument. So, I chucked away my waiting job in PJ Clarke's on Third Avenue, packed our belongings and, without giving it much more thought, followed my husband to Rathluirc, County Cork.

***

When I got this waitressing job at The Sugar Sugar Café, I learned that members of Alcoholics Anonymous get coffee for half price. This is because Jerry, the boss, is also a member of the brotherhood. Those were his instructions on my first day at work.

'How will I know who's in the brotherhood and who's not?' I asked him.

'You'll know them when you see them. Mostly

14

they've got bad skin and really awful haircuts, and they look like the kind of guys with a lot of regrets,' Jerry said.

'Okay, I'll be sure to watch out for that,' I said.

Funny thing I noticed about Jerry—every time we get to talking a while, his accent will change and he begins to sound like he's Stateside too.

'Anything else?' he said.

'Yeah, what kind of tips can I expect to make?'

Jerry laughed so hard I thought he was going to choke to death, right there in front of me.

Then, another fine day, not long after I got this job, Billy's father walked out on us. Just like that. He left a note on the kitchen table, beneath a can of Batchelors baked beans. I think the note was really for his mother. He took all our savings and the car, leaving me and Billy stranded in Rathluirc, with nothing but each other.

***

Jerry gave Billy a present of a mongrel pup. It was a scrawny thing that Jerry promised wouldn't eat much. He said I could take all the scrap food I wanted from the café. Jerry was all wrong about the dog's appetite. It might have been a scrawny thing, but it ate like a pregnant horse.

From the beginning, Billy and that dog couldn't be separated. Lemme tell you, the dog has had a freakish calming influence on him. Billy talks to the dog more than he talks to me. I watch them play together in the fields at the back of our house. Since getting that dog Billy has even started doing some chores. And his teachers don't phone me so much to come get him from school.

Yesterday, as a birthday surprise, I took Billy to see *The Hunger Games* in the movie theatre in Blackpool, Cork city. As a special treat I bought two jumbo tubs of buttered popcorn and a couple of sodas.

In the darkness, I hustled him down the aisle towards the screen, away from the other kids, and corralled him into the seat next to the wall. Billy loves the movies, especially the toons and gore movies. He had his fingers in his mouth for most of *The Hunger Games*.

Then, before I could stop him, he leapt out of his seat and cried out, 'The hunger games have begun, the hunger games have begun!' I reached to grab him, but he was already gone from me. Billy kung-fu kicked into the air shouting, 'Happy hunger games!'

The other children pointed and laughed at him as he ran up and down the aisle karate chopping invisible warriors. And for shame, I sat down again, lowered my head and ate my popcorn. I watched the rest of the movie and pretended he wasn't mine.

***

The brass bell over the door goes *fring fring*, and I turn to see an old lady push herself into the café. She's built like a midget wrestler. Lidl bag in each hand, she sways around, searching for a seat. That's the trouble when there are so many empty seats: nobody knows where to sit. I give her the laminated menu and I stare out at the trucks passing along Main Street. I'm thinking that, after she's eaten her regular scone, she's gonna head straight for the ladies' restroom, like she always does. Then she's gonna pee all over the floor and after she's done, I'm going to have to clean it all up.

As always, the old lady wants a pot of weak tea and a plain scone. She never looks at me when she speaks. I write up her order and study the bald patch on her head. Her hair is three different colours. I pop a frozen scone into the microwave and make the tea.

When I pick up the cold coffee mug from the schoolboy's table, he glances at an opening in my blouse.

'Still here, hon?' I say.

No response.

Anyway, the bell goes *fring, fring* again and in comes Vincent. He takes a seat at his usual spot—table 8. He lays the *Racing Post* across the tabletop like it's a map. There are little lumps of bathroom paper stuck to his throat, like he has leprosy or something. Over here they call Vincent a 'gentleman farmer', which means he owns a couple of acres of scrubland that makes no money and he lives off a cheque that comes from somewhere over in Europe. He has a roll-up cigarette dangling from his mouth.

'Don't even dream of lighting that thang in here.'

'Coffee please, Alice, and be nice to me this morning,' Vincent says.

'Sure thing,' I say.

'No, Alice, I mean it. I'm not feeling great today.'

'Really, hon?'

'Not good at all, 'tall,' he says.

'Aww, poor baby, got that ole vodka flu again,' I say.

***

Last Christmas, after we'd closed up for the holidays, Jerry and I went for a drink in The Auld Triangle bar on Main Street. Jerry wore those tight blue jeans of his, the ones with the bell-bottom flares. He wore a check shirt and winkle-picker shoes. All he needed for an Idaho barn dance was a ten-gallon Stetson. I was still in my skanky café uniform. Jerry drank sparkling water and I was throwing back a local take on a vodka sea breeze. Jerry kept checking his Amish sideburns in the Johnnie Walker bar mirror.

Soon Jerry and I got to comparing the sexual needs of men and women. Jerry said that women have no idea of the powerful urges lurking within a man. He said that men are victims of their own biological make-up. 'Suppose that a guy gets into a lift and at the next floor this beautiful specimen of a woman gets in and the lift goes up. Well, by the time that lift has reached the seventh floor, that guy is ready to have sex with her. It's not our fault. It's just our nature.'

Jerry looked at me as if to say, 'What do you make of that?'

'Hon, I'm surprised it would've taken that long.'

A pal of Jerry's yelled out 'Happy Christmas!' from the far end of the bar counter. A guy in a three-piece suit that went out of fashion sometime before they invaded

Vietnam.

'Jerry, Jerry, happy Christmas, aul' stock,' the guy yelled again.

'Yeah, happy Christmas,' said Jerry softly as he fiddled with his shirt buttons.

The guy raised his glass in a toast to Jerry. Jerry's response was to barely raise his glass of water off the counter.

'Merry Christmas to you, sir,' I yelled to the guy.

The guy pushed his way through the crowd and down to our end of the counter.

'Jerry, Jerry, Jerry,' he said. 'Please introduce me to the lovely lovely lady.'

'The lovely lady is called Alice and she's from New York,' said Jerry.

'I'm from Buffalo but it's close enough.'

The guy's name was Vincent. His eyes were bloodshot and wild. He held my hand tenderly in his and for a moment I thought he was gonna kiss the back of my hand.

'Alice is married with a child,' Jerry announced.

'Not anymore I'm not. I mean I have a son but I'm not married anymore.'

'Me neither,' said Vincent.

'Say, it's kind of late, what time does Billy normally get to bed at?' said Jerry.

'I'm sure the sitter will take care of Billy,' I snapped back.

Vincent insisted on buying me a Baileys shooter and Jerry left the bar complaining about the noise.

I explained to Vincent how I came to be living in Ireland. When I told him about Billy, I got all lonesome for the kid in a stupid kind of way and almost started weeping right there at the counter.

Vincent could never be convicted of being handsome, but then neither could I. When they played Bing Crosby on the bar stereo, Vincent and I sang along. He told me about his horses and offered to let me ride one of them. He said Billy would love his horses. Like he'd know what my Billy would love!

'So how do you like working for Jerry?' said Vincent.

'I love Jerry,' I said, 'but not in a romantic way.

21

Jerry's a great guy.'

'Jerry is a gas man,' said Vincent.

'A gas man? Jerry's a gas man? What the fuck is a "gas man"?' I asked.

Vincent laughed.

I wished I wasn't still wearing my stupid ugly work uniform. I hoped to Christ that Vincent couldn't smell the cooking oil from my clothes and hair. In the ladies' restroom I bought disposable toothpaste and a packet of condoms. I brushed my teeth. The hot water faucet wouldn't work. I tried to clean 'top and tail' using damp bathroom paper, though I still hadn't made up my mind.

The cab that pulled up outside the bar was the size of a small school bus. Vincent introduced me to the cabby as 'Alice the American waitress'. The cabby's name was Paudie. Only in Ireland do you have guys named 'Paudie'. I couldn't get my tongue around all those vowels, so I called him 'Paddy'. Every time I called him 'Paddy'—and I did it a lot—they laughed and Vincent corrected me.

'It's Paudie. "Paw" followed by "dee". Isn't it, Paudie? Isn't that how you say it? Try it again, Alice. Say "pa", as in "you shot my pa" or like, like "my dog has four paws", and then just say "dee", and put the two of them together and then you have it.'

'Okay, I think I got it. How you doin' up there, Paaaadeee?'

The rain poured down from the black sky, ratatating against the windshield. I snuggled into Vincent's chest. The dirt road leading to his house was full of holes and ridges. The cab hopped out of one pothole and landed in another. It was as if the road was juggling with it. Every time the cab hopped, the cabby shouted, 'Jesus, Mary and Joseph'. Vincent bounced up from his seat and almost landed on my lap. He had no change, so I paid the fare.

'Alice, won't you please excuse the mess? I gave the maid the evening off,' Vincent said.

The house was big, old and damp. Vincent went looking for a bottle of tequila. I sat on the bottom steps of the stairway and tried not to think about Billy.

'You live here all alone?' I shouted to the darkness.

'*O Sole Mio*,' he sang back.

'Awful big house, he's got an awful big house,' I said to myself.

I took off my sneakers and smelled their insides.

Vincent appeared from nowhere and clinked together two green long-stemmed wine glasses.

'I have salt but I seem to be just out of lemons,' he said.

'You ever been married, Vincent?'

'Once, I was married once.'

'Once is enough for anyone,' I said.

'Amen to that.'

The damn tequila burnt like hell. I followed the first hit with another and it didn't burn anymore. Vincent sat on the steps beside me. He put his arm around my neck and pulled my face towards his and there was no going back after that.

It was sometime after two when I saw the headlights of Paudie's cab bouncing down the dirt road, coming to collect me. It was still raining.

'Do you mind if I smoke, Alice?' Paudie asked, as I got into the back.

Hank Williams was playing on the radio. The moon was big and bright and I sang along to 'Lovesick Blues'.

Standing beneath the street light outside my house

I straightened myself out as best I could before turning the latch on the door. Mrs Roche, the sitter, was reading a magazine on the couch. She gave me one of those extra-long sighs of hers. She never said anything when I was a little late. She didn't have to.

***

Anyway, now Vincent pretends he's forgotten everything that happened that night but I know he knows, and he knows that I know he knows, and it gets all Donald Rumsfeld after that. What can you do? You gotta keep on moving, that's what you gotta do.

Vincent orders scrambled eggs on toast without looking up once from his paper.

Fring, fring! Burnt Toast comes into the café with a copy of *The Irish Times* tucked under his arm like it's a sergeant major's baton. He settles down at table 5. I pass him a menu but I know already what he wants: 'Two slices of burnt toast, two slices of crispy bacon and coffee'.

Burnt Toast rummages through the pockets of his denim jacket and places items he finds on the table. It's like he's going through a security check. A cell phone, a pack of Gitanes, a box of matches. When he finds a red little notebook, he sighs with relief. He thumbs through the

25

notebook until he finds the page he's looking for. Then he stares at me while I give his order to Carl. He writes something in the notebook. It's like he's drawing pictures of me or he's writing something about me.

***

Last night, while at work, I got a call from Mrs Roche. Something was wrong with Billy. He'd gone for a walk with his dog and when he came home there was blood on his hands. She said he was upstairs in his bedroom with his head under a pillow, refusing to talk to her. She started calling me 'Mrs Woods' even though she is years older than I am.

'Is he hurt? Is Billy hurt?'

'I don't think so. Look I told you, Mrs Woods …'

I had another two hours left on my shift at the café.

Mrs Roche brought the phone up to Billy. His voice was broken and he whispered something about the dog. I couldn't make out what the hell he was saying about the damn dog.

Mrs Roche took the phone back and said Billy was frightening her. She started coming on all, 'I'm not able to deal with this. This is not part of the job. I didn't sign up for medical emergencies.'

'Is he hurt? Is my Billy hurt?'

'I don't think so. Look I told you, Mrs Woods ...'

'Is he bleeding? Where is he bleeding?' I asked in the calmest voice I could muster.

'I'm not sure that I know that,' she said.

'I'm on my way home.'

I grabbed my coat and hurried out the door leaving Carl to deal with the customers.

When I got home, Mrs Roche had already gathered her knitting basket and pattern magazines. I crawled onto the bed beside Billy. There were bloodstains on the pillow and the sheets. At least he hadn't wet the bed. I searched his body and I couldn't find a single cut or bruise.

'Where did all this blood come from?'

No response.

'Where's the dog?'

No response.

I brought him to the bathroom and made him take a shower. I know how he hates for me to see him naked and for once he didn't put up a fight.

I changed the sheets and pillowcases. I washed his hands in Dettol and hot water. I tucked him into bed and lay beside him stroking his face with my fingertips. He lay so still. I wanted him to lie still like that forever.

'Billy, please tell me what happened to the dog?'

'Got run over by a white van. It was an accident. Nobody else saw it. I picked him up in my arms and brought him over to O'Brien's field and buried him under a pile of stones. Mom, I even put a cross there.'

Billy talked as coolly as if he was describing something on a cartoon show he'd seen on television. I lay there on the bed, watching over him, stroking his face, knowing he was lying but not knowing why. I promised him Jerry would get him another dog soon.

'Okay, Mom,' he said.

I kissed his forehead.

'It wasn't a rock that done it, Mom—it was a big white van,' Billy said.

I looked out his bedroom window. It was still bright outside: the summer nights are long here. I left his bedside light on and his bedroom door open. Then I went into the kitchen, cut myself a slice of birthday cake and fixed myself three fingers of Jim Beam.

***

Burnt Toast starts waving the menu at me like there's a chance he'll get lost in the crowd.

'Tole ya, hon, be right with ya,' I say.

Carl slaps the cowbell to let me know Vincent's scrambled eggs are ready. The radio beats out some commercial jingles and I feel very tired.

I watch Vincent mark out the day's runners at some race meeting. The unlit cigarette is still dangling from the corner of his mouth.

'*Fring, fucking fring!*' The kid who was cutting high school steps out onto Main Street. He stands on the pavement with his full satchel hanging from his shoulder. He looks up the street and he looks down the street, not sure where to go next.

The little old lady starts rummaging through her groceries for something and Carl slaps the cowbell once more.

He shouts out, 'Alice, Alice, get over here.'

Carl always has to say my name twice when he gets in a panic.

It's pushing on for 11.45 a.m. and it starts to rain again.

Two

Carl O'Shea, Chef

2012

Player: Carl O'Shea

Carl O'Shea, Chef

This is how you make French toast, Carl O'Shea style. Break three fresh eggs into a Pyrex bowl, add seasoning and a little Golden Vale pouring cream. Grate eight ounces of fresh Parmesan cheese and add to the eggs and cream. Add a pinch of cinnamon. Get a bulbous whisk and whip the shit out of the mixture. Cut two slices from a decent loaf of bread and remove the crusts. Let the bread soak in the bowl of egg mixture while you put a large frying pan on the hob. Toss a knob of Kerrygold butter into the pan and let it melt until it begins to bubble, then add the soaked bread. Fry both sides until golden. Remove from the pan and add a desert spoon of tomato ketchup and a desert spoon of French mustard. Fold into the shape of a Swiss roll. Now eat.

Jerry comes in the back door of the kitchen. He's wearing wellingtons and carrying three plastic bags bulging with flat-leaf parsley. Jerry has started to grow his own in his back garden, along with carrots and butterhead lettuce. He wants us to start using the parsley as a garnish in the café. He says that the parsley garnish will give a classy feel to The Sugar Sugar Café. The only thing that would give a classy feel to The Sugar Sugar Café is a jerrycan of petrol and a match. Jerry is standing over me, waiting for me to admire his garden produce. I remove my sailor cap and scratch my head. All I'm really thinking is he has enough parsley here to feed France.

'More parsley, Jerry? That's exactly what I was looking for,' I manage to say, even with some French toast still in my mouth.

Jerry drops the bags by the bain-marie. He takes the bunch of delivery dockets skewered to the nail block. 'D'you sign for all these, Carl?' he says, with his back to me.

'Every single one.'

He changes the radio station from Kiss FM to Lyric FM. He goes upstairs to his office, his feet stamping on the floorboards. I take a fistful of parsley, stuff it in a colander and give it a good spraying with the power hose by the dishwasher. The parsley will dry by the open windows. I change the radio back to Kiss FM and turn up the volume.

Jerry wants us to start putting specials on the menu in the evening. He wants things like chicken Kiev and chicken Maryland, and doesn't want any more Captain Birdseye. Jerry wants us to reach the 'family market'. I've no problem with specials on the menu. I can cook chicken Kiev. I can cook chicken Maryland. I can cook chicken fucking George, if I have to. But get me some more help in the kitchen. I can't do it all on my own. I tell Jerry we need to hire a commis chef. He says that we already have a commis chef. He's talking about me. How do you like that? I'm thinking about quitting this job. It's far too stressful. Way too many chiefs in this place, and only one fucking Indian.

I empty the colander of parsley onto a red plastic chopping board that has caught fire so many times it looks like a map of Spain. I catch opposite ends of the knife, the tip and the hilt, and using a rocking movement, I start to chop. Up and down and right to left and back again. Never once letting the tip of the knife come away from the chopping board. Right to left and back again. Just like we were taught in the merchant navy. The parsley begins to smell like a freshly mowed lawn after it's rained. I gather it into a new pile and chop all over again, using that same rocking motion. Rocking and chopping, just like we were taught.

Alice is standing by the back door, watching me. Hard to tell how long she's been standing there. She's smoking a cigarette. She inhales inside the kitchen but exhales through the back-door screen. Like that makes all the difference.

'Jerry's here,' I say to the parsley.

'I met him,' she says.

'Okay.' I stop chopping and quickly put my sailor cap back on.

'Carl, I just want to say that I'm sorry about last night.'

'It's okay, no matter.'

'No, it does matter. I was worried about my kid.'

'I understand, Alice, really I do. You had to stay home. You were worried about Billy, and you had to stay home.'

She pulls back a strand of hair that has fallen out of her slide. She catches the slide in her mouth while she fixes her hair. I could watch her do that all day long.

'Did you wait a long time for me?' she says.

'I waited a while, you know. I had a pint while I was waiting. There wasn't much happening like. I had a pint and then I waited, and then I went home.'

We both hear the café's doorbell ring. Alice winks at me and throws the cigarette into the alley. I chop more parsley. Rocking and gathering. Just like we were taught.

Alice has an order for poached eggs with hollandaise sauce. Poached eggs are not a problem for Carl

O'Shea. Poached eggs are on the menu at The Sugar Sugar Café. Hollandaise sauce, however, is not on the menu. Hollandaise is a problem—a big fucking problem. Alice stands there with the order docket in her hand, looking like a schoolgirl in the principal's office.

'Jesus Christ, Alice, do these people have any idea how long it takes to make hollandaise sauce?'

'I don't know, Carl. I never ask them.'

'You start with a reduction of vinegar, see, and that will stink out the whole fucking kitchen like, for sure. Then you have to separate your eggs, the yolks from the whites. Then you put the egg whites in the fridge where they'll stay for a week before you throw them out. You float a Pyrex bowl in a pot of boiling water and add the egg yolks, and then you add the vinegar reduction to the egg yolks. And then after all that, you have to drip feed the egg yolks with slices of warm butter. It takes forever like. And I mean fucking forever. That's why people won't cook it at home and that's why the fuckers come in here, looking to see if they can get some, even when it isn't even on the fucking menu.'

'Can I take that as a "no" so, Carl?' says Alice.

'Well, if you need me to elaborate?'

She's gone before I can say anymore. I return to the

mounds of parsley and start chopping again. Anyway, there's something else we learned in the merchant navy—when you're carrying too much weight on board, you must throw something over the side or else you're going to sink. So, when I'm certain no one is looking, I open the food bin and toss half the bag of parsley in there. Then I toss in a couple of slices of bread and a couple of sheets of tinfoil until the parsley is completely hidden. With Jerry, you just never know.

Alice is back by the hatch, watching me chop the rest of the parsley.

'That lady will take bangers and mash instead—will you put 'em on?' she says.

'Bangers and mash? Sure, no problem. It's never a problem for the chef when it's on the menu like.'

'And hon, I need two crispy rashers for Burnt Toast.'

'Two crispy rashers coming up.'

What Alice needs in her life is a man like me. I could take care of her. I could take care of Billy too. I know I could. I don't know what she sees in that langer Vincent. He's no better than her ex-husband. But first I need to get my own restaurant. Property is cheap now. Everybody is selling and nobody is buying. Alice and me could work together in a place of our own. Maybe an Italian restaurant with red-and-white checked tablecloths and a good selection of wine. And decent bread—people love decent bread. You can't get decent bread in this country unless you make it yourself. With Alice out the front charming the customers and me in charge of the kitchen, how could we go wrong?

The sausages are almost done when Alice appears back at the hatch. 'I got a live one here, Carl. He wants a T-bone, well done. His words were, "Very, very, very well done". You got that, hon? Was there three "verys" there? Because that's what he said—he said "very" three times.'

'He said "very" three times?'

'He sure did. You okay, Carl? You don't look so good today.'

'I'm okay, Alice.'

'Are you still upset about last night?'

'Last night? No, no, no, last night was no problem for me.'

'Was it the hollandaise?'

'No, it's nothing.'

Alice catches hold of my hands and pulls them closer to her face.

'You burn yourself tonight hon?'

38

'It's nothing,' I say.

''Cos I got hand moisturiser if you need it?' she says.

'I'm fine, Alice, I'm fine. You tell him the steak will take at least twenty five minutes?'

'I tole him already. He's okay with that.' Alice turns away from the hatch and as she walks away the cheeks of her ass wobble from side to side. It's like ping-pong up her skirt.

The raw T-bone is big, almost fills the frying pan. I sear both sides as quickly as possible to keep the juices in. Then the microwave pings. The mash potatoes are done. I plate up and then wipe the grease stain off the plate with the corner of my tea towel and lay it on the hatch for Alice. I nearly forget to garnish the mash with parsley sprigs.

Once I get the rashers frying I put my face up to the dinky little fan that Jerry bought in Lidl to feel the cool air. I take my cap off and wipe my forehead with the tea towel. The radio has been playing holiday songs all night and I feel a powerful thirst for porter.

Alice places an order for three plates of chips and a mixed grill. I turn the deep fat fryers up and go get a lamb chop in the walk-in fridge.

Jerry has a problem when it comes to spending money on the café; he's especially allergic to spending money on the kitchen. We could do with a new deep fat fryer and the back oven hasn't worked in months. Sometimes the walk-in fridge is warmer than the kitchen. What Jerry doesn't realise is that the kitchen is the engine room of the café. If it's not working in the kitchen, then nothing is working.

When the rashers are good and crispy I plate them and mop the oil off with the tea towel. Then I lay the plate on the hatch and give the bell a slap.

'How's that mixed grill comin' on?' Alice calls out.

'Any minute now.'

Everything is under control. The rashers, black pudding and the lamb chop are sizzling under the grill and the T-bone is smoking on the pan. The mash is spinning in the microwave. The chips and sausages are dunked in the deep fat fryer and swimming about like they're having fun in the ocean. Even the gravy sauce on the hob thins out without any fuss. I slap the bell again and Alice appears at the hatch like she's been waiting there all along. She carries away the mixed grill plate, the mash bowl and the chips.

When the T-bone's done I arrange it neatly on an oval dinner plate. At the last minute, I remember to sprinkle everything with Jerry's home-grown parsley. Then I lay it on the hatch for Alice and slap the bell one more time.

It's time to wipe down and I start by carrying the bowls of breadcrumbs and beer batter back to the fridge. I spray the stainless steel countertops with soap and wipe them down. The sink is full of dirty pots and frying pans. They've been steeping there since I clocked in. Another night of steeping should do the trick.

If there's one thing I have to do soon, it's get a foot on the property ladder. Unless you get a foot on the property ladder, the next rung will always be out of reach, because the next rung of the ladder is always going to be higher. Jerry has property in Turkey—two apartments in a seaside town. He bought them off a catalogue. Jerry's never even been to Turkey and now he owns a part of it. I've been everywhere around the world and I own none of it.

Then I pour a half-cup of Robert Roberts and carry the coffee outside to the alley. Leaning against the skip, I find the cigarette in my pocket that I stubbed out earlier. Jerry's Hiace is parked further back the alley. I go and sit inside the van. The car keys are behind the sun visor. The radio is tuned to Lyric FM. I change the dial to Kiss FM and crank up the volume full blast. Then I turn the engine off and when I flick it back on again, some death metal rock

41

concert blasts from the speakers. I turn the engine off once more and put the keys back.

'What are you doing out there in the dark, hon?'

'Nothing, Alice, I was doing nothing.'

'You sure?'

'Sure, I'm sure.'

Alice holds the T-bone between her fingers like a used tissue. 'He says the steak is overcooked.'

'For fuck sake, he said he wanted it burnt.'

'I know, hon, but now he says that it's burnt too much,' Alice says.

'He wanted his steak very well done. That steak is fair well done. That's what he ordered like.'

'I know, Carl. Now he says that this steak is overcooked.'

'Overcooked? He wanted it overcooked. Three times he said "very".'

'It's people, Carl, what can I say? He wants another steak.'

'Let me get a look at this guy, which one is he?' I follow her back inside and I lean up over the hatch. I still can't see the guy. I stand on an overturned stockpot so that I can see all the way to the front door.

'Which fucker is it?' I ask.

Alice tries to nod her head discreetly to her left.

'Is it the langer reading the newspaper?' I ask.

'The very one,' says Alice.

'He fair looks like an out and out complainer to me.'

'Well, I guess he's fussy about what he eats.'

'I don't know, Alice, some of these guys complain about the food just to get a free meal.'

'Well, hon, you know what they tell them in Harvard Business School?' says Alice.

'No, what's that they tell 'em?'

'The customer is always right. They tell them in Harvard that the customer is always right.'

'I bet it was a customer who came up with that one,' I say.

'Look, Carl, it might be best to get this guy fed and out of here, before Jerry comes downstairs.' She glances up towards the ceiling.

'I don't have another T-bone. Might have some rib-eye in the fridge. Will the fucker eat that?'

Alice goes and consults with the customer and is soon back at the hatch. 'That's great, Carl—he'll eat the rib-eye. You're a sweetheart. Only two "verys" this time. He wants it very, very well done.' She winks at me and smiles. When Alice smiles, The Sugar Sugar Café lights up like it's Grafton Street on Christmas Eve.

In the walk-in fridge, I find a rib-eye steak. I walk to the back of the fridge where we keep the milk and I stuff the rib-eye down the front of my chef's pants. I give 'Fagin' a good wipe with it. Then I shove it down the back of my pants and I give my hole a good old rubbing about. Standing all day in the kitchen can chafe the tops of the thighs and the hole area. They used to call this chafing 'the wolf' in the merchant navy. I have to say pressing a raw rib-eye steak between the cheeks of the hole can be as comforting as a finger of Sudocrem.

Standing by the hob, I throw the steak into the frying pan. The gravy sauce is thick as jelly. I pull a booger out of my nose, a good meaty one, and add it to the gravy sauce. All of a sudden, I feel like whistling. I don't know why. I'm usually not a whistling kind of a guy.

Alice has the radio tuned to a country and western station. I hate country and western music but if it's okay with Alice it's okay with me. I whistle as I cook the guy's steak. I catch Alice staring at me.

'How's that steak comin' on?' she says.

'Not ready yet, Alice. It's only well done. We have to make it "very, very". We don't want to get it wrong a second time like.'

'Sure, sure,' she says.

'Oh yeah, that's a fact. We must try and satisfy the customers. That's what they teach 'em at Harvard. "The customers are people too", and that's what Jerry says.'

'Carl … about last night, I had the sitter organised and I had my make up on and I was sitting in my car and about to drive off, and Mrs Roche—that's the sitter—calls me back because Billy had started crying. He wasn't feeling so well. He was sweating. He had a temperature. A hundred and two.'

'Is that high? That must be high because boiling point is one hundred.'

'Well, yeah it's high.' Alice frowns. 'I had to sponge him with cold water. He fought me all the way. He's real strong and when he doesn't want to do something, well, it can be a struggle, you know? My arms are bruised from him pushing me and pinching me. But we got it down.'

'Good. Billy is a good lad.'

'His dog died you know?'

'I know, you told me.'

'Got run over by a van,' she says.

'I know.'

'Quiet tonight,' she says.

'Sure is, Alice.'

'You know, Carl? Maybe we could try again sometime. I mean, if you want to. I don't know if you want to.'

'We could give it another go, if you want, Alice. I think we could do that.'

'Okay, better watch that steak—you don't want to burn it, only two "verys", remember?' She winks at me.

'Sure thing.'

I find that T-bones and fillet steaks are best cooked as quickly as possible under a high heat, so as to seal in the juices. But rib-eye steaks are different; rib-eye steaks should be cooked slowly and they are best eaten almost raw.

I hack up a good ball of phlegm into the pot of gravy and give it a good stir. The steak is ready to go. Alice smiles appreciatively when she sees the steak decorated with parsley along with the fresh chips. She smiles at me and I stand on the overturned stockpot again and watch as Alice serves up the steak to the fucker. He leans back and starts pointing at the steak and talking about it, like he's the king of beef. Alice looks back towards me. She bites a lip. She offers him a weak smile. He pushes the plate away. He pushes back from the table. He pulls a flat cap onto his head with great purpose and leaves.

Alice carries the plate back to the hatch.

'What the fuck happened?' I say.

'Guy said he wasn't about to eat somebody's road kill.'

'The ignorant fucker. The out and out bollocks. I fair can't believe the langer said that?'

Alice cuts off a piece of the beef with the tip of the steak knife and dunks it in the gravy.

'What are you doing?' I ask.

'Guy didn't touch it. I hate to waste food. Especially waste food like steak.'

'Stop, stop, Alice, Alice, you can't eat that?'

'Why not, hon?'

'I don't know ... you just can't ... maybe some other customer might want a steak ...' I pull the plate away.

'There's nobody here looking for steak,' she says.

'I'll eat it. I want the steak. I cooked it. I want it. I'm the chef.'

Alice brings her fingertips to her mouth. She looks like a child whose doll I stole. I take the meat in my mouth and close my eyes. I hold the meat on my tongue. The gravy spreads all along my tongue. I can taste the pepper corns and beef stock and nothing else. My toes curl. I don't know if I should swallow the meat without chewing or hold it in my mouth until I can spit it out when she's not looking. I open my eyes, Alice tilts her head at an angle. My stomach heaves like I'm about to give birth through my mouth. A customer calls Alice for their bill and I lift the plate off the hatch and rush for the back door. Out in the alley, I spit the piece of meat onto the ground. The French toast and all the coffee I've drunk that day comes gushing out of me as I vomit against the stone wall. I toss the plate along with the steak into the skip.

'You out here again, Carl?' says Alice from the back door. Her tone is hostile.

'I'm here.'

'Everything okay with you tonight?' she says as she comes closer to me.

'Everything is fine.' I wipe my mouth with the tea towel.

'You sure you're okay?' she says.

'Just getting some air. Listen, I was thinking of going for a drink after I finish up here,' I say.

'You were?'

'Sure, after all the excitement here tonight, I was thinking that I could fair murder a pint of Beamish.'

'Billy is waiting for me at home.' She folds her arms across her chest.

'Sure, sure. Alice, I'm sorry about the steak … I shouldn't have what I said.'

'Look hon, I better get back to the customers.'

It's warm outside in the alley but the clouds look dark and heavy with rain. The moon is nowhere to be seen and there are no stars. The stink of burnt oil and rotting food drifts over from the skip. My stomach hurts from all the heaving, and I'm hungry for food while at the same time revolted by the thought of it.

I need something plain to eat, something plain and wholesome that won't make me sick.

This is how you make bread and jam, Carl O' Shea style. Take two slices of white sliced pan, you could use Brennan's or Pat the Baker. Remove the crusts with a sharp knife. Smear room temperature Kerrygold butter evenly over one side of both slices. Add a couple of dollops of Folláin blackcurrant jam to one slice only. Be careful not to apply too much jam or it will overpower the butter. Place the jam slice of bread neatly on top of the buttered side of the other slice and cut into four triangles. Now eat.

Three

Pictures of Jesus

A story from the past

Player: Alice Woods

Pictures of Jesus

I was tending bar in PJ Clarke's on Third Avenue when I first met my husband, Mattie. He came into PJ's with his construction buddies, and they'd drink pitchers of beer like Prohibition was about to return in the morning. Sometimes Mattie would pick up the dirty glasses for me and carry them back to the counter. He had that easy Irish charm and, of course, the accent. It was the accent that got me first. I couldn't get enough of that sing-song voice of his. We started going out and soon enough we moved into an apartment together—first floor in a brownstone in Greenwich Village.

Mattie asked my dad over the phone for my hand in marriage, the way they do it in Ireland. Dad's response was to ask Mattie if he was having any luck with the green card application.

One fine morning we got married in the City Clerk's Office in Manhattan. It was a small affair. Mom drove from Buffalo that morning. Dad didn't feel well enough to leave the veteran's hospital. My bridesmaid was a fifty-six-year-old burnt-out waitress named Rhonda. Mattie's best man was a Puerto Rican sheet metal worker named Louis. None of Mattie's family flew over, though he swore he'd invited them all.

We worked hard. We drank our fair share. Then I got pregnant when I wasn't so careful. Lemme tell you, Mattie did not want me to keep the baby. And he's the one who's Catholic. My folks were never big into religion and neither am I but, like I told everybody, I was keeping my baby.

Billy was born on a beautiful Sunday morning in February 2000. Six pounds and six ounces and greedy for me. Looking at my baby, I could not believe that this beautiful gift from God came about from me and Mattie screwing around. I know how biology goes but this just blew my mind. We called him Billy, for my dad's younger brother, William F. Dodds, who was still in the navy at the time.

Billy cried a lot as a baby. He cried so much we couldn't get babysitters. Lemme tell you, Billy didn't sleep much either. Even as he got older, one hour of sleep did him fine and for the rest of the night, he'd rattle the bars in his crib like a prisoner in a jail. When Billy turned six, he was diagnosed with ADHD. That changed everything for me but it changed nothing for Mattie. I could see beyond the tantrums and the tears and somewhere there was my beautiful baby boy. When the tantrums really got going, Mattie reached for another can of Bud.

***

Mattie convinced me that Ireland was the best place to raise Billy. Mattie could be awful convincing when he wanted to be. My mom drove us to JFK in her broken-down Mustang. She was wearing her ridiculous rabbit-skin coat and giant sunglasses. Throughout the ride to the airport, Mattie suspended all hostilities towards her. Mom sent him on a fruitless errand to buy her a pack of Luckies and she gathered Billy and me into a group hug.

'Now, Alice honey, you do know this'll all end in tears, don't ya?'

'Please, Mom … please … not here, not now,' I said.

'No, Alice, let the truth come out. Ireland! For Chrissakes, it's not even England.'

'Do ya love your grandma, Billy? Do ya?'

'I'm going on a plane, on a plane, a plane,' said Billy.

Mom took off her sunglasses and hugged him. 'I'm never gonna pay a visit—ya know that, right? I never been there and I never going there … to Ireland … and I don't care even if one of ya ups an' dies on me. Got that, Alice?'

I kissed her and hugged her tight.

'Tell Mr Wonderful he can hold onto the Luckies,' she said as she turned and left the departures lobby of JFK.

I took Billy for a walk around the airport to tire him out. Mattie sat in the bar because he has a fear of flying. Billy and I took photos of each other making faces in the photo booth. Mattie sat by the window on the plane and Billy sat between us. Billy played with his dinosaurs. Mattie tried to fall asleep. While the flight attendants went through their safety routine, Billy amused some of the passengers by mimicking the attendants' demonstration.

Billy kicked the seat in front and a purple-haired old lady leaned back and gave Billy the big eye.

'*Let's get this baby off the ground,*' said Billy imitating the pilot.

'Not so loud, Billy,' I said.

The old lady smiled and I fed Billy a grape.

'When's the movie on, Mom?'

'Soon.'

'What time is soon?'

'Soon is soon.'

'Is soon in five minutes?' Billy asked.

'Can you count the number of passengers wearing neckties? Tell me how many people are wearing neckties. Can you do that?'

Billy knelt up on his seat and got busy counting. I got two minutes out of that one before Billy screamed, 'Eight!'

'Can you count the number of kids on the plane?'

'No.'

'Can you count the number of ladies on the plane?'

'No.'

Billy went to the restroom twice in twenty minutes. Then he sat on my lap and we wrestled with each a while until he stopped trying to get away from me. Mattie slept by the window seat and Billy resumed kicking the seat in front.

Soon the old lady called the flight attendant, who came and told me Billy was upsetting other passengers. She went to her station and found an Elmo doll for Billy.

'I'm sorry, miss,' I tried to explain. 'He's upset. He's never flown before.'

'I want Buzz,' said Billy.

'Buzz is in the suitcase and we can't get him until we land.'

Billy tossed Elmo across the aisle of the plane. The attendant's mouth tightened. I tapped Mattie on the arm. Mattie released a snort.

'Little boy, are you hungry? 'Cause it's nearly dinner time,' said the attendant.

'It's not dinner time yet,' said Billy.

'It is here, son,' she said.

'No, it's not. No, it's not. It's not dinner time until seven.'

'Can you keep it down, Billy?' I said. 'Calm yourself, let the lady do her job,' and I began to massage his neck.

'I got this, ma'am,' said the flight attendant.

'No, you don't,' I said.

'Little boy? We have to serve the passengers their dinner now because, well, they're hungry now and if they don't get their dinner, they'll get mad with us. Do you understand now?'

'I said it's not dinner time,' Billy screamed, and tried to kick the pop-up tray.

The old lady with the Marge Simpson hair stood up in the aisle.

'That child is bad. You ought to smack that child,' she said to me.

'My child has special needs, ma'am,' I gripped my arms around Billy's body.

'Special needs? Special needs? Honey, we all got them!' said the old lady.

'I'm sorry, ma'am. We didn't mean to spoil your flight.' I turned to Mattie. 'You gotta help me here.'

'Please take your seat, ma'am,' said the attendant to the old lady.

'If yo' child is special needs, how come he don't got no chair?' said the old man sitting with the old lady.

'It's not that kind of disability. Billy has a chemical imbalance. He'll be good. I promise. He'll crash soon and fall asleep, I promise. Just give him five minutes and he'll be okay. I promise. I promise.'

'He'll be grand,' Mattie piped up.

I took Billy back onto my lap and began to massage his arms and legs again.

The pilot instructed the passengers to buckle up: there was turbulence ahead. The attendants hid behind a curtain. The plane shuddered and seemed to drop from the sky. It was like the air went out of a balloon. The emergency lights came on.

'Holy fuck!' said Mattie.

Billy wrapped his arms around my neck. I could hardly breathe.

'I got you, Billy. Don't you worry none.'

Billy let out a piercing scream. I covered his mouth with my hand. The plane rocked. Two attendants came running to us.

'He's okay, he's okay. He's just frightened,' I said.

'He's upsetting the other passengers, ma'am.'

'He'll be okay. I promise. I promise.'

The plane settled again and the attendants looked at each other for suggestions, with their blonde hair and their perfect teeth and their bright eyes. They looked at me like

I was the queen of white trash. Billy stopped thrashing about on my lap and started to sob quietly.

'Look, he's okay now. See—we'll be fine. I'm sorry for the trouble we've caused you.'

They returned to their stations.

The captain announced in a deep and cheery voice, like he was the Marlboro man, 'The turbulence is over, folks—you can go back to enjoying your flight.'

'Do you think we've crossed halfway yet?' said Mattie in his half asleep voice.

'I don't know, I guess maybe, why?'

'If we're more than halfway, they won't turn back and throw him off,' said Mattie.

It took a while but Billy did eventually fall asleep in his seat between me and Mattie, clutching the Elmo doll. Mattie stared out the window seeming to count the clouds bringing us closer to Ireland.

I went to the restroom and sat on the toilet for so long one of the cabin crew came knocking on the door to see if I was okay.

***

We moved in with Mattie's parents, Bridie and Ollie. The five of us lived together in a three-bedroom council house on Bishop O'Brien Terrace in Rathluirc.

Hot water was on ration like we were back in World War II. Everybody was allowed one bath per week. There was no such thing as a shower. The hot water tank was stored in the airing cupboard—or as Bridie called it, the hot press. This room was always locked and Bridie had the only key.

Mattie had forgotten to tell me about the rain. Over here it can rain every day for weeks on end. But worse than the rain was the damp. Everything in Bridie's house was damp: the walls, the windows, the bed clothes, everything. The only heating sources were two coal fires and an electric bar heater that Bridie carried with her from room to room, like it was an oxygen tank. When it finally stopped raining the rainbows appeared in the sky. Billy and me had never seen so many rainbows. Sometimes there were three and four rainbows in the sky at the same time. They seemed to reassure me that someday our luck would change.

Bridie and Ollie didn't share a bedroom, so Billy had a cot in a corner of our room. That caused more difficulties, of the marital kind. Now, I'm the kind of girl who likes to make a little noise when it's time to make a little noise. But I knew for sure, with the pictures of Jesus and all the different popes on the walls, that Bridie wouldn't appreciate that kind of thing.

Mattie got a job as a courier with DHL. I didn't go looking for a job until I was sure Billy had settled into his new school. When Mattie came home from work he'd make us all laugh with his stories of delivering the wrong parcels to people and getting lost on top of mountains. Sometimes if he'd had a really long day at work he'd bring home a box of chocolates and I'd take them to our room and eat them in bed.

Having spent every St Patrick's Day for most of my life on Delaware Avenue, Buffalo, usually freezing to death, I thought at last I'd see the real deal—an *Irish* St Patrick's Day parade. I bought a green blouse and skirt in Dunnes Stores and I dressed Billy in a nylon leprechaun suit, complete with red Wolfman beard. Bridie, Ollie and Mattie pinned tiny pieces of shamrock to the collars of their coats and went to Mass.

We stood on the Main Street, outside The Auld Triangle Bar waiting for the parade to start. Crowds gathered along the sidewalk. Billy was jumping out of his skin. Then Mattie said, 'Fuck this' and went inside the bar for a pint.

Leading the parade down the middle of Main Street was an old man dressed in a green smock and paper hat, wielding a staff like he was Moses trying to part the Dead Sea. Following behind him, a geriatric brass band murdered a couple of Benny Goodman tunes. The band couldn't play and march at the same time, so they stopped marching every twenty yards or so to play a bit. The band was followed by some schoolgirls perishing with the cold in tiny sailor suits and pantyhose. There's something so not right about schoolgirls in sailor suits and pantyhose. They were followed by three milk trucks, a gas truck, a couple of hungry-looking greyhound dogs, and another milk truck. It was all over in ten minutes.

'That's it? You gotta be kidding me?' I said to Billy.

'That's it,' said some guy in a denim jacket standing beside me.

'That can't be it. There has to be more. Jeez, parade in New York takes four hours. Someone please tell me there's gonna be more.'

'This isn't New York,' says the guy, with a shrug.

By then the romantic ideals I had of Ireland were

long gone. And my heart no longer skipped a beat whenever I heard those magical Irish accents and I turned to this guy with his black spiked hair and I stared at him a long time. 'I know it isn't New York' I said through gritted teeth. He offered me a Gitanes cigarette but I just grabbed Billy by the arm and dragged him away.

It started to rain again and I could have cried as we walked back to Bridie's house. When we got back to the house Bridie and Ollie were already positioned in front of the TV watching other parades from around the world. Mattie stayed in the pub and got shit-faced—and all I wanted to do was call Mom and tell her that she had been right all along about this country.

***

Bridie's house reeked of gravy. She must have had the same brown pot of Irish stew on the boil for the entire time we lived with them. My body is no temple, but I couldn't eat in that house. Whenever it was time for dinner, I pretended I'd eaten already or I wasn't feeling well and later I'd get Mattie to take me to The Sugar Sugar Café for some fried chicken and French fries. That's where I met Jerry, the owner, and got myself a waitressing job.

Mattie and me worked all the hours we could. We

were saving for a place of our own. I believe it was the very thought of having a place of our own that kept me from going insane. I would have preferred us to go back to New York or even Buffalo, but Mattie insisted Ireland was the best place for Billy. He talked about the schools and the medical care and the free college education.

***

One evening, while watching the soaps, Bridie said, 'Would you ever tell me what's wrong with your child?'

'There's nothing wrong with Billy.'

'The child never stops fidgeting,' said Bridie. 'It's unnerving to watch.'

'Then don't watch.'

'Yes, but it's not normal, is it?' she said.

'Billy is a child—everything is normal for a child.'

'What I mean to say is that … sometimes he acts like he's been … hypnotised—like with the telly—and when you call him, he can't hear you and he won't budge for you, and other times he's hopping out of his skin and can't sit still. That's all I'm saying.'

'That's just Billy being Billy, and don't ever say he's not normal in front of me again.'

Bridie took a long drag on her cigarette and stared at the TV. A large cloud of smoke exited her nose.

***

Sometimes Mattie would take me for drives in his delivery van in the evening. It was just about the only time we got to be alone. We'd check out all the new housing estates being built—they seemed to be popping up everywhere. We'd bitch about our jobs and we'd bitch about money, then I'd bitch about his mom; he'd bitch about Billy and that always hurt.

We took to making out in the back of the van, up in the Ballyhoura woods. Among the brown paper parcels, I could make all the noise I wanted and I sure did. I screamed louder than thunder.

Then one fine day when I couldn't take the hygiene situation in Bridie's house anymore, I went and bought all manner of cleaning utensils and soaps down at the Rathluirc Co-op Store. I filled every one of Bridie's black pots with boiling sudsy water, vinegar and baking soda, and left them steeping in the backyard. Then I mopped, brushed, washed, scrubbed and disinfected all the walls and flooring of the kitchen. I cleaned out the refrigerator, the cooker and defrosted the ice box; there were things in that

65

icebox that must have been in there since the war in Vietnam. I had to use a paint scraper to get the crud off the linoleum floor.

Bridie just stood by the door watching me, smoking her Rothmans, barely containing her anger. She studied my every move. Down on my knees with a deck scrub in my hands, I scrubbed the bathroom clean. I even used a toothbrush to clean the grouting on the bathroom tiles.

Finally she spoke. 'You think yer better than us, don't ya?'

'No, ma'am.'

'You do too, all you fooking Yanks are the same. You come over here telling us what to do and ye haven't a fooking clue. Not a fooking clue. Just look at the big arse on you. What's my son landed himself in? Not a fooking clue have you.'

I stretched my foot back and shut the bathroom door in her face.

Bridie refused to talk to me for weeks after that. Mattie begged me to apologize to her. He said that the day might come when we might need her help.

'It's her house—we're the guests,' he said.

'And there I was thinking we were family, what a putz.' I didn't care. I didn't want her help.

Ollie never said anything much about anything. He was always busy in his shed, fixing things. I gotta say that I saw a lot of broken toasters and irons going into that shed, but I never once saw anything fixed coming back out of it.

Mattie took on an extra job driving a cab on Saturday nights. He didn't punch out until 4 a.m. He spent most Sundays in bed, reading the papers. We saved every single cent we could and put it into the credit union, trying to scrape together enough money for a deposit on a new house. But every time we saved enough for the deposit, the price of houses went up. We could've bought a small apartment in Greenwich Village for the money that the realtors wanted for a four-bedroom townhouse over here.

Some days, when I collected Billy after school, we'd drive out the Golf Road to where they were building a new housing estate called Wiltshire Lawns. We imagined what it would be like to live there when it was finished. We'd sit in the car, making up stories about our new neighbours. They were always nice and had lots of kids and toys, and invited us around all the time for cookies and cocktails. Billy and me would put on Irish accents. Billy sounded like a miniature Barry Fitzgerald; I sounded like I'd taken a toke of helium. Sometimes, Billy would shout to the Polish carpenters, telling them to be careful building that house; that house was going to be our house.

It's all still like a dream to me. One day the three of us were living in Greenwich Village and then, before I know it, I'm sitting in a tiny Fiesta with my son, parked by a building site in the middle of nowhere, with the rain pelting down onto the hood.

I still marvel at the rainbows over here but I don't think I'll ever get used to the rain.

Four

Rain on a Tin Roof

A story from the past

Player: Carl O'Shea

Rain on a Tin Roof

I spent ten years of my life as an ordinary seaman in the merchant navy. I reckon I was seasick for the entire ten years. Most of the time I worked as a chef but sometimes I worked below deck as a greaser. The pay wasn't any good but I always had money, because out on the ocean there was no place to spend it.

I reckon I've been to every corner of the world at least once and forgotten most of it. One port town looks a lot like another, and I'm not the kind of fella who collects mementoes.

The last time I was at sea was in 1999. I was on board an oil tanker called the *Elysian*. We were on a tour from Liverpool through Panama for a discharge in San Francisco. The crew were mostly English, Greeks and Egyptians. I was the only 'Mick'. We'd docked a week in Panama City for repairs and were preparing to set sail again in the morning. I was on shore leave and making my way back to the ship when it started to piss rain. I didn't have a coat and my chinos were splattered with water and mud. I saw the light of a cantina. The words 'Bar Manny' were painted in huge red letters on both sides of an open door. I wasn't in any kind of hurry, so I stepped inside.

There were black and white stencil portraits of Che and Fidel behind the bar. And photographs hanging on every wall, of bikers and biker-chicks displaying ornate tattoo jobs. A woman peeped through a white pearl-beaded door curtain. She smiled at me. Her hair was scrambled yellow and her teeth were Hollywood white. She beckoned to me to come inside and take a seat. I climbed down the concrete steps that led to the bar counter. Bamboo chairs leaned against white plastic garden tables, waiting for customers. I sat up on a stool by the counter. She was wearing a man-size white T-shirt and cut-off denim shorts. She wore no shoes. She could've made the cover of *Penthouse* magazine.

I let up a Marlboro. She snapped open a bottle of Balboa beer for me. She flipped coins from my pile of change on the counter, like she had another job as a bank clerk.

Outside, the rain came down on the tin roof like it was the end of the world.

I dried my face and hair with a paper napkin and took a look around the bar. I saw, reflected in a Brahma beer mirror, a man at the back, hunched over a fruit machine.

71

'Gringo, gringo,' he called.

I ignored him. I didn't want any trouble.

'Come, sit to me, my friend,' he said, pointing towards a table.

One thing I've learned in the merchant navy is that any fella that calls you 'my friend' sure as hell ain't your friend.

'Señor, please sit to me,' he said.

I looked up at the portable telly behind the counter and watched Al Gore being interviewed on CNN. The sound was low and the ticker tape announced that civil war had erupted somewhere in South America—not in Panama, but someplace else.

The barmaid put another bottle of Balboa in front of me. I studied her mouth. She should've been in London or Milan, selling yachts and Rolexes to rich assholes. She looked at me like I was Brad Pitt and Santa Claus all rolled into one. She flicked through the TV stations and banged the side of the telly with her fist to clear the picture. Some South American soap opera began playing out on the black-and-white screen.

'You are American, no?' the guy persisted, and

pulled the arm of the fruit machine into loading position before delicately releasing it.

'No,' I said, without turning around. The rain stopped. Squiggling noises emerged from the heart of the fruit machine. I looked out at the mud street and watched a black and red cockerel strutting along with his chest puffed out, like he was on his way to work.

'Canadian?'

'No.'

'English? *Si, si, si,* you are Englishman.' He slapped the side of the fruit machine, sure of success this time.

'No.'

And so it went.

It grew dark outside, faster than I've ever seen a day turn to night. All of a sudden, there were no shadows anymore.

I should've been back on board the *Elysian*, reading one of my porn mags and listening to The Pogues on my Walkman, but I ordered another Balboa instead.

The guy shouted something to the barmaid and she put a shot glass in front of me and filled it with Mexican tequila. She poured until it overflowed onto the counter. She laughed again and spoke to me in Spanish and it sounded to me like she was an angel singing my favourite song. Her huge brown eyes held mine. I saluted her with a raise of my glass. I stood up from the stool and poured the tequila down my throat. It burnt like fuck and ran wild through my stomach. I held back the urge to cough. She took another lump of change from the pile in front of me.

'Dutch? You Dutchman?'

'No.'

He sat down at a table at the back of the bar.

I touched the money belt underneath my Hawaiian shirt. Every penny I had in the world was in there. You couldn't leave anything of value in your locker on board the *Elysian* and expect it to be there when you got back from shore leave. That was just the way it was in the merchant navy.

An old Indian woman came into the bar and sat down on a rocking chair. I could smell shit off her all the way from the other end of the bar. Her skin was like torn tyre rubber. She glared at me, pulled a shawl over her shoulders and began to mumble crossly about something. The bar girl called her 'Momma', but she looked too old to be her momma.

'Please, Señor, sit to me.' He tried once again.

And I did.

We shook hands ghetto-style. This was Manny. This was his bar. His skin was speckled with some rash and he smelled of Old Spice cologne. I have always hated that smell. Manny called me 'Carlito'. He called the bar girl 'Betty'. When he said her name, he said it like there was a *h* and a *w* somewhere in the middle of the word. He wore yellow Nike sneakers, surfer pants and a torn, soiled white vest.

Manny offered me a shot of tequila from his own bottle. There was a worm sitting at the bottom—it looked like a tiny turd. He slapped my thigh just like he had done with the fruit machine. I offered him a cigarette; there wasn't enough room on either of his arms for another tattoo.

'You are Frenchman?' he said.

'No, I'm Irish.'

'What is Irish? Where is this?' he said.

'Ireland, *Irlendas*, in Europe.'

'Ahhh, Irelands, yes, yes, *si, si, si,* Belfast, boom-

boom!'

'That's right: boom-boom.'

Betty brought over a plate of cured hams and fried yuca. Her skin was coffee brown all the way around. She spoke Spanish with Manny and took away the empties. Grandma spat a mouthful of phlegm onto the dirt floor. Manny ate quickly and encouraged me to do likewise. He spoke with his mouth full of mashed yuca.

'What you do in Panama?'

'I'm on a merchant ship.'

I nibbled the ham and studied Betty's body while she polished glasses behind the counter. Manny licked his fingertips as elaborately as if he was about to perform a magic trick. He tried to explain the curse of Yankee imperialism that had befallen all of Central America. I didn't care about Yankee imperialism, and I didn't care that Betty knew I wanted her, and I didn't care if he knew that I wanted her either.

'Our General Noriega, you know him? This one is a great man. A great man. He help people of Panama. The people love him. I tell you, Carlito, I love this general. Look at the Yankee, look what he done. The CIA? You know what I say to CIA? Fuck you, CIA!'

'Damn right, fuck the CIA,' I said. 'A bunch of out and out langers.'

'Fuck them good,' he said.

'Amen to that,' I said.

The ham tasted of nothing but salt. The yuca tasted like deep-fried parsnips.

'Carlito, my friend, you want nice tattoo? I make one so nice for ten dollar,' he said.

'Maybe later.'

'Carlito, you like another one beer?'

'Sure.'

'Betty, come to us. Bring beer.'

Manny removed a chain from around his neck and released a red and black Mickey Mouse pendant. He unscrewed the figurine in half and poured some coke onto the back of his wrist. He snorted loudly, leaning back on his chair and raising his chin up, like he was expecting a shave. Grandma stood up and shouted Panamanian curses at both of us from across the room.

Manny slapped the tabletop and laughed at her. His

teeth were yellow all the way back. 'We must be careful, she like to kill me, maybe she like to kill you too,' he said.

He offered me a toot. *When in Rome*. The coke scorched the inside of my nose and pushed the alcohol fog aside. I was ready to march for Ireland.

'Good shit, no? Carlito?'

'Very good shit.'

'Is primo candy,' he said.

'Manny, my good friend, let us cut to the chase, like,' I said.

'*Si, si,* we must do this, my good friend Carlito.'

'How much for the woman?'

'One hundred dollar,' he said.

'Ten dollars. American dollars, with a nice picture of Alexander Hamilton on the front,' I said.

'Carlito, you no understand, everything in Panama is American dollars.' He laughed.

'I'm not a rich American tourist. I'm a sailor like, just a working stiff like you, Manny.'

'*Si, si, si.* This one prima chick. Eighty dollar, go on, take another look at her. Maybe you miss something last time you look.'

And I did. I stared at her as she watched the soap on the TV. I wondered how much of our conversation she could understand.

'As you can see, Carlito, this is hot chick.' He laughed like a donkey.

Betty led me by the hand through the beaded door to a bedroom upstairs. I sat on a thin-mattressed bed and watched her do a line of coke off a silver hand-mirror. Her head jolted as she snorted back the coke and jolted again as it hit its target. She offered me a toot and I took one more hit to get the blood flowing. She turned the radio on. Some South American disco trash boomed around the room. I took off all my clothes but left on my money belt. I lay back on the mattress and watched her lift off her T-shirt. I couldn't believe my luck.

Two hours later, I woke beside her. I checked my money belt and watch. There was still time to get a taxi back to the port before the *Elysian* set sail. I pulled back the sheet and reached out to touch her. She turned on her side. I traced the tattoo of an image of Jesus on the cross on the small of her back with my fingertips. I stroked her hair. She brushed my hand away like it was a fly.

I fetched some bottled water from the dresser and watched the stars through an open window. I got into bed beside her again and pressed my face against the nape of her neck. Her skin was soft and hard at the same time. Her hair smelled of coconut oil.

'Can I ask you, Betty? Is that your real name? Betty?'

She had her back to me and didn't answer. She didn't even turn around.

'Do you understand any English at all?'

There was no response.

'You are the most beautiful thing I've ever seen.'

She began to snore.

***

Later in the morning, when I woke, she was gone. Manny was in his boxers by the bar.

'Betty back later. You owe me money, gringo. You stay long time,' he said.

'There's no problem, Manny. I got dollars, like.'

I sat by the bar counter. Manny began the new day with a little toot off the back of his wrist. He charged me an extra twenty dollars for staying the night and ten for a breakfast of onion tortilla and a Budweiser.

'Gringo, I hope you not love her,' he said.

Out of habit I checked my watch. I knew my ship was long gone—they wait for no one in the merchant navy. I sat at the bar counter and watched CNN while I waited for Betty to return.

'How about I give you a nice one tattoo?' Manny asked.

'No thanks.'

'*Si, si, si,* nice one tattoo special for you,' he said.

'Not today.'

He showed me his arms. 'You see this one tattoo— this one is eight ball. Difficult to make the eight ball. This one tattoo is the broken chain, see here, this one. You can only have this one tattoo if you go to jail. It is the law. You ever were to jail, Carlito?'

'No. They haven't caught me yet.'

'They caught me. Two times they caught me. Fuck the police and the CIA. See this one tattoo here? This one tells the world of my love for my mother.' He blessed himself and said some short prayer in Spanish. 'You are a sailor, Carlito, but you have no tattoo? How can this be? It is like a farmer without a horse.'

'I guess I never got around to getting one, like.'

'Well, Carlito, my friend, you can get one now, you come to right place, ha, ha! Here is tattoo heaven.'

He pointed to the photographs on the walls of bikers and their tattoos.

'Manny has all the tattoos you want. Manny is number one tattoo artist in all South America. Is me, Manny.'

'That right?'

'*Si, si*, damn that right.'

'That's good,' I said.

'Once there was this one guy. This one guy in Chile. This one fucking guy in Chile. You know Chile?'

'Been there once, I think.'

'This fucking guy was special artist. I don't know this guy name. He was famous for tattoo. You know what I saying?'

'Sure.'

'The gringo Yankee bikers say to me, "Manny, you

good tattoo artist, but this one guy in Chile is more good." So, no more Yankee biker business for Manny. What Manny gonna do? Fucking guy … This a big problem for Manny. So I drive down to Chile to find this fucking guy. I drive Chevrolet. You know Chevrolet?'

'Sure, I know Chevrolet.'

'Is good car, no?' he said.

'It's a good car alright.'

'I drive down to Chile. Betty come too. She like my car. I find this guy working a beach outside Tocopilla city. I see his work. This guy is an artist. I mean a fucking artist, Carlito. You know what I say?'

'Sure, guy's an artist.'

'You know about artists, Carlito?'

'No, I don't.'

'This one fucking guy was … *excelente*, the mostest, the best I ever did see.'

'Okay.'

'So I take out my gun and I shoot the some-bitch in the head. Now Manny number one again in all South America.'

'Jesus!'

'Gringo bikers come back to Manny for tattoo.'

'Jesus.'

'Ha ha, no, Carlito! I is joking, my friend, I is joking. You need more relax, Carlito,' he said.

'How long more before Betty gets here?'

'Soon. Betty here soon. You want tattoo now?'

'Maybe later.'

'You know, Carlito, a woman, she wear the make-up—the lipstick, the perfume—but the man, he can do nothing, except wear tattoo. Today Manny have special offer Betty Boop tattoo cost twenty dollar. What you think about that? Nice surprise for Betty. Sit to me.'

And I did.

Betty returned sometime in the afternoon. She and Manny argued in Spanish while I sat by the counter and sipped my beer. Betty went upstairs. Manny motioned to me that I could follow her. Then Betty and me picked up where we had left it the night before. And so it went.

In the evening Betty cooked chicken with rice. Manny played the fruit machine and I snorted a line of coke through a twenty-dollar bill. There wasn't much in the way of customers and I never saw the old Indian woman again. Manny sang songs in Spanish and in English, and Betty danced to the music on the radio. When it was my turn to sing, I stood as straight as I could in the middle of the bar and sang the only song I know all the words to: 'The Rose of Tralee'.

'Bravo!' said Manny.

'Bravo!' said Betty, clapping her hands.

***

A couple of days later I found myself lying face down in a water fountain near the soccer stadium. It could have been morning; it could have been afternoon. There were children laughing and shouting at me. I was shivering in the sun and could hardly breathe. I had no money, no watch, no shirt and no shoes. Some children threw stones at me. I could hardly stand. The sun was blinding and I struggled to keep upright. I stumbled away from the fountain and away from the beating sun. I didn't know where I was going but I kept shuffling along regardless. I didn't look back, even when hit on the side of my head by an empty Pepsi bottle. The earth scorched the soles of my feet but I kept on walking.

I found a stone church and went inside to sit in the

85

coolness of the shadows. The church was small, white and bare. It occurred to me that there is a lot in Panama that is small and white and bare. On the walls hung the black wooden carvings of the Stations of the Cross, shining like marble. I squeezed myself into a pew beneath a statue of some black saint. I'd never seen a statue of a black saint before. I tried to recall a prayer I'd learned in primary school but couldn't.

Flashes of the previous few days came back to me. Mostly, I saw images of Betty's mouth. I knelt by the altar and lit a candle I couldn't pay for. I was hungry, aching for sleep and beer, and I curled up on a bench and slept.

The next morning a priest woke me. He was clean-shaven, pale-skinned and had perfect teeth. He looked about nineteen years old. I told him I'd been robbed by a taxi driver and left stranded by the side of the road. I could have laughed—I could have cried. His name was Padre Juan. He spoke English like an American. He gave me coffee and bread in his rooms at the back of the church. The bread was so hard I couldn't chew it. He gave me slippers and a check shirt to wear. The slippers were too small for me and the shirt stank of sweat. He wanted to talk about James Joyce and *Riverdance*. What the fuck do I know about James Joyce and *Riverdance*? I sat on a wooden stool in his kitchen and listened to his stories about his college days in New York City, and all I could think about was what were the odds of finding the one priest in South America who didn't drink or smoke? When he offered to hear my confession, I declined.

'What was the name of that Irish boxer who beat Pedroza?' he asked. 'The little one with the old ladies' moustache, who never stopped fighting?'

'I don't know, Father.'

'You must know. He was World Champion.'

Later Padre Juan phoned the Irish Consulate in Panama City. He smiled a lot while he tried to explain my situation. I spoke to an Irish guy who had adopted a thick South American accent. I told him the same story I'd told Padre Juan.

Padre Juan's beat-up Toyota pickup was parked in the shade of a palm tree, with the windows down. The seats were burning hot. A child, wearing a Lakers T-shirt, stood in the street staring at us, while the priest helped me into the pickup—Padre Juan 'capturing another gringo devil'. Rosary beads hung from the rear-view mirror, swinging from side to side. Every house in the neighbourhood was single storey, with whitewashed walls and orange-tiled roofs. Twice I asked him to pull over so I could puke by the roadside.

The Honorary Consul of Ireland had offices several floors above the Bank of Boston in the gleaming downtown city centre. In the foyer Padre Juan shook my hand and wished me luck. He gave me enough small change for a coffee and a burger at the airport.

The lift was air-conditioned and panelled with mirrors. I held onto the brass railings as the doors closed. Indian pipe music played as the lift ascended. I remembered the boxer's name—it was McGuigan but it was too late now. I stared at the red carpet. I would've puked again but there was nothing left inside.

They were waiting for me in the Consul's office, two civil servant types—nice suits and nice manners—but I knew what they were thinking the minute they saw me. Both were Irish but spoke Spanish to each other. They issued me with an emergency passport and gave me a one-way plane ticket to Heathrow and a connection on to Shannon. I had to sign a promissory note to say that I would repay the money for the flights when I got the chance. I don't think they were too worried about the loan. I think they may have been a lot more nervous of the idea of me staying on in Panama City.

At the airport I walked past armed custom guards with their mirrored sunglasses and German shepherds. I was wearing the priest's check shirt, my own torn pants and a pair of shoes borrowed from the Honorary Consul. I held my hands in the air, as if surrendering, waiting for them to question me but they waved me through.

I watched soap operas on TV while waiting to board. I drank water from the taps in the toilet and bummed a cigarette from an American tourist.

Later I followed a line of British tourists across the tarmac in the searing heat and onto the plane. The air hostesses looked at me, as if they knew every rotten thing I'd ever done in my life. There were no smiles for me. Nobody said, 'Enjoy your flight, sir'.

I took refills of every freebie they were dishing out: coffee, pretzels sandwich rolls.

In Shannon, crowds were gathered behind railings in the arrivals lobby. It was like somebody had won something and now they were coming home, victorious. I stumbled through the shrieks and hugs. Just as in Heathrow, the crowd opened to make space for me to walk through, like I had some kind of disease. I wandered around the airport until I found a seat nobody else wanted.

The tannoy announced flight arrivals from Paris, Berlin, Rome. My stomach grumbled. I scratched my body, first my head and then my face and then my stomach. I scratched my legs so hard they began to bleed. People began to notice me so I went outside.

It was raining, a soft summer kind of rain. Brightly lit taxis were lined up to take people wherever they wanted to go. I looked across the vast car parks trying to figure out how I was going to thumb my way home to Rathluirc. I followed behind a group of happy-to-be-home passengers pushing their heaving trolleys towards the bus shelter. The trolley wheels clanked along the crooked pavement. Someone tossed a half smoked Gitanes cigarette onto the footpath and I waited until they were long gone before I picked it up.

A plane came thundering overhead and I suddenly realised that all I had left to show for my ten years in the merchant navy was a Betty Boop tattoo that covered the length of my thigh.

Five

Brief Encounters

2012

Player: Burnt Toast

Brief Encounters

Every morning begins the same. I give the bus driver my monthly ticket and he checks the expiration date. He never salutes me or smiles or acknowledges my presence. The other commuters in line behind me try to move me along. I recall reading somewhere—in *The Ticket*, perhaps—that people over forty who still take the bus to work were failures in life. I wonder if that still applies, now that the world has reached the tipping point in the supply of fossil fuels and capitalism, as we know it, may be at an end.

A passenger plumps down on the seat beside me. She tries to make more room for herself by nudging me towards the window. I turn my face to the glass, but I can taste her worn sneakers and her damp woollen cardigan. On days like these, I curse the smoking ban.

The bus is 'chock-a-block', as people used to say. Steam rises from passengers, like it's some early morning fag sauna in San Francisco. As I wipe a clear spot on the window with my elbow, my thoughts turn to today's task— a review for my film blog, *Brief.Encounters.com*. This afternoon is my last chance to see *Seven Psychopaths* at the Kino cinema. It'll entail some skulduggery at my current employment benefactors, but that's part of the job of blogging. I wriggle my red Silvine memo book out of my coat pocket and read yesterday's attempt at an opening paragraph for the review:

> *Regular readers of this column will be aware of my penchant for afternoon cinema-going. The afternoon is truly the only time to see a film: the pensioners never distract you with high fives or hellos, there are no youths attempting to mate, and sometimes you have the theatre to yourself.*

I draw a line through the word 'truly', and begin reading over again*: Regular readers of this column …* It is of no consequence that I am about to review a film that is being withdrawn by its distributors. It is not my purpose to provide a public information service—I am writing this blog for posterity. If John Citizen wants cinema information, he can read the advertisements in the *Evening Echo*, like everyone else.

After re-reading the same paragraph a half dozen times I'm unable to add more lines to the introduction and the review reaches a standstill. The rest will have to wait until I have actually seen the film. I stuff the notebook back into my coat pocket and listen to the coughing and spluttering of fellow passengers on the way to Cork.

*****

I recall, many years ago, when I was an occasional undergraduate in University College Cork, that there used to be cinemas situated all across the city centre. Each of them had only a single film screen, except for The Lee on Winthrop Street. Sometimes a cinema showed the same film for weeks and weeks. The Lee had an additional mini-theatre that held about twenty people. I saw *Emmanuelle* there—it was that kind of cinema. It's gone now, replaced by an arcade of one-armed bandits.

My favourite cinema was The Palace on McCurtain Street. Its full name was 'The Palace of Varieties'. It was a throwback to the music halls, with its thick red carpet, big bucket seats, gold-leaf plaster columns and velvet curtains that drew apart to reveal the screen. The cinema theatre was replaced years ago by a real theatre. Now they have live actors prancing about on a wooden stage.

*****

Anyway, whenever a film comes to town that simply must be viewed, I tell my current employers, Rattigan, Palmer and Hodge, that I have a toothache that needs urgent attention from my personal dentist (is there any other kind of dentist?). My current dentist is a Dr Schmidt of Patrick Street. That is Schmidt with a *d*, by the way. I like the Teutonic effect that oozes from the name Dr Schmidt— authoritative, precise and with all the possibility of serious pain. My employers were impressed, at first anyway, by my choice of tooth doctor. However, I fear that, perhaps due to the frequency with which by now I have referred to the doctor, the novelty has truly worn off.

The office manager, 'Nurse Ratched', has begun to feign an interest in some German *Vorsprung durch Technik* for herself. So far, I have managed to put her off the idea by implying that Herr Doktor's hygiene is wanting. Lately, however, she has found the impertinence to quiz me further, casually enquiring about the credentials, qualifications and worse still, address, of said Dr Schmidt.

I have come to the conclusion that perhaps dentists should properly be referred to as 'tooth technicians', rather than 'healthcare professionals'. There are even some rogue dentists who consider themselves to be the equivalent of medical doctors. These are probably the most dangerous kind. The kind that believe a PhD allows one to designate oneself as 'doctor'. After all, dentists merely cater for one part of the body, a small area in relation to the entire corpus.

In my own field—accounting—fully qualified accountants are referred to as 'accountants' and part-qualified as 'accounting technicians'. And then there are those poor souls—such as myself—who are not qualified for anything at all, and are referred to as 'bookkeepers'. These are the poor souls who shall inherit so very little.

In the office, I slump into the chair and log on to the computer. The computer, struggling to come to life, bellows like a donkey dying of consumption. I'm working on some farmer's annual accounts; he has twenty-two different bank accounts and I have to balance them all. He has money transfers coming in and going out of each bank account at an alarming rate. I have not figured out why he needs twenty-two bank accounts, and I have not figured out whether he himself understands what is happening with his money. I have spent three whole weeks working on bank reconciliations for this farmer, and the accounts still do not balance. Rattigan, Palmer and Hodge will not make a cent on this client's fee.

Una glides into the office and throws herself down on her chair. That is Una with the long legs and short skirts. Today she is wearing trousers, even though girls are not allowed to wear trousers in the office. The senior partner, Mr Rattigan, is offended by many things, including atheists, people of colour, poor people and Revenue Commissioner people. He is also offended by the two other senior partners, Palmer and Hodge. But most of all, he is offended by ladies in trousers.

Poor Una has 'office exit trouble,' in that she cannot pass her final professional accountancy exams with the CPA and get the hell out of this office. With Una's consent, I have been assigning some of my work hours onto one of her larger clients.

'How you doing?' I say.

'How the fuck do you think I'm doin'?' she drawls. 'My phone ring yet?'

'I'm making myself a coffee—you want one?'

'You're a dote—two sugars and no milk, and don't get caught.'

I try not to make the stairs creak on my way to the basement kitchen, which is no bigger than a phone booth. I fill the kettle and slip into the lavatory while waiting for it the kettle to boil. There is a rusty iron bathtub sitting against the wall in the lavatory. The taps in the bathtub are stuffed with toilet roll.

I keep alert for signs of Nurse Ratched. She has never taken to me, ever since that day she caught me walking out of the lavatory with a copy of *The Bonfire of* the *Vanities* under my arm. When I suspect that the kettle may have boiled, I open the bathroom door. Una's pink mug has scenes of cavorting cats; my mug has a scene from *The Wild One*. I make two cups of Red Rocket's finest. The coffee smells like hot washing-up liquid. *I love the smell of napalm in the morning …*

I make a dash upstairs, carrying a mug in each hand. Una is on the phone, discussing a client's year-end stocktake with Mr Rattigan. The Child of Prague looks down from the wall, smiling kindly on both of us.

Una closes her eyes, stretches along her chair and pretends to lick the phone. She rubs the phone against her breasts and gyrates her hips. Then she returns the phone to her ear. 'Yes, Mr Rattigan,' she moans deliciously.

Jimmy Brazil's huge head appears; he stares through the glass in the office door. Jimmy looks like Homer Simpson sporting a Lord Lucan moustache. Jimmy must be sixty bells. I cough to warn Una, but she has already pushed the phone down the front of her trousers. Jimmy taps on the glass door and smiles at Una. She knows her little peep show is going to get back to the senior partners. Little Jimmy (as he is known) is the office fink. Little Jimmy is like me, unqualified, and has given up on the idea of ever being qualified. He has already spent a good share of his life trying to get through his CPA exams. He holds the office record of sixteen attempts.

I dial Nurse Ratched's office. I try my best Tony Randall. 'I feel a terrible toothache coming on.'

'But you just got here,' she says. I do not like her tone of voice.

'I'll try to last till lunchtime.' I add some spittle sound effects over the phone. 'I'll do my best to get an afternoon dental appointment.'

'I guess if you're in pain, you're in pain. Will you try your regular dentist on Patrick Street? The one above The Body Shop?'

'Ah, I will.'

The office girls assemble by Una's desk for their lunch break. Rosie and Lily are the office typists, Ciara and Theresa are the junior accountants, while Miss Woulfe is the receptionist. Miss Woulfe is the oldest virgin in Cork.

Una licks tomato sauce from her fingers. The smell of chips and vinegar fills the room. I sit by my desk and sip tea and continue to work on my introduction to my film review of Seven Psychopaths:

It is always a poor sign when films arrive in a blaze of publicity and worse still, when the film promoters take out advertising space on television.

'I hope you're not writing anything about me,' says Rosie.

They all laugh, like she has said the funniest thing in the world. I catch Una's eye and blush. I try to add to the review but each time I write something down, somebody makes a comment. I get my coat and leave the office by the back door.

Lunch is a sandwich roll in Fellini's on Carey's Lane. The roll is so full of ham, grated cheese and celery salad that the filling spills onto the plate. It is delicious. They provide free newspapers for customers and this makes the lunch affordable. The coffee tastes rich and strong. It has an accompanying mini chocolate biscuit; it's the most luxurious thing I have ever tasted.

Strolling down Patrick Street, I gaze through the shop windows. I stop outside Lunny's camera shop. Each year cameras somehow manage to become smaller but better. I wonder how they do that. Smaller but better, year after year. I see The Body Shop on the opposite side of Patrick Street. I smile as I stroll along. Above the shop on the second-storey floor, the faded painted sign: 'D.W. Schmidt Dental Practitioner'.

Then I see Nurse Ratched, standing by the entrance door to The Body Shop. I duck behind a white Volkswagen.

She is wearing a dark grey business suit and her famous black leather jacket, the one that makes her resemble a well-fed SS officer. She checks her watch. She goes into The Body Shop. Then comes back out again. She paces about, like she's waiting for a late bus. Then she takes off in a hurry, down Patrick Street in the direction of Grand Parade—the same direction as I'm going.

I'm following her, but it would appear that she is trying to follow me. She walks at an angle, with the determination of a Lenten preacher, but all the grace of a retarded mud-wrestler. I can't keep up. Soon I'm out of breath. She crosses Grand Parade by the boarded-up Capitol cinema and I cross by Daunt Square. She slips down the alley and comes to a halt right outside the Kino cinema. I hide behind a black Hiace van. She goes inside and starts talking to the old guy behind the ticket desk. They seem to talk forever. I never liked that old guy, always quick with a smart comment about my having 'another day off work' and I could often detect an unpleasant body odour.

Fuck! I can't remember Nurse Ratched's real name. Is it Josephine or Daphne? It is definitely something old school.

She emerges from the cinema, looking like Darth

101

Vader's mother. She has her own personal dark cloud hanging over her. I scramble back behind the Hiace. She tries to cross to my side of the Washington Street but the traffic is thick. My only hope is that she will be run over by a truck. But there is no such luck.

By the court house I sneak around the side of a furniture delivery van until I'm standing on the road and I'm watching her through the side window. Then I'm nearly sideswiped by a bus. It is my bus; that is my driver. *Now* he recognises me. *Now* he is willing to salute me with a honk of the horn and a thumbs-up. I wave him away but he persists with saluting me and this time with a louder and more sustained honk. Nurse Ratched scans the street. I turn down Cross Street and hide in the doorway of St. Francis's church on Liberty Street.

I phone Una—no answer. I phone the office.

Miss Woulfe answers the phone with that phoney West Brit accent of hers. 'Rattigan, Palmer, Hodge and Co, registered auditors. This is Miss Woulfe speaking. How may I help you?' She puts me through to Una.

'I'm fucked! Nurse Ratched was waiting for me outside the Kino. She tried to bushwhack me. She knows. She knows about Dr Schmidt. I'm fucked, I'm truly fucked—I'll be fired as soon as I get back!'

'You sure got yourself in a tight spot, dote.'

'Any ideas?'

'You could come back to the office before her and say that the toothache is gone and now you don't need a dentist.'

'No, no, she knows, Una—she was waiting for me, it was a trap and now I'm fucked.'

'Leave it with me, dote. Phone me back in ten.'

I light up a Gitanes. I hurry along Liberty Street, cursing my luck. If it wasn't for bad luck, I'd have no luck at all.

Una phones me from the office lavatory using her mobile. 'I got you sorted, petal. Get yourself up to North Main Street. There's a dentist there by the name of Bill Smith. You have an emergency appointment at 2.45 p.m. Get a tooth pulled, dote, you got them to spare. Make sure you get a receipt though, with the time, date and the dentist's name on it.'

'I don't know about that, Una. Having a tooth pulled is so much pain. I'm not built for pain.'

'Well, dote, that's the price.'

'I don't know, Una—it'll never work.'

'What does work?' she says.

As I cross North Gate Bridge, I watch the river

103

rushing by. I debate whether to take the bus home to Rathluirc or go back to the Kino and watch the film anyway or get a tooth pulled. I feel like emptying my lunch into the river.

I receive a text from Una: *She's back.*

The brass plate on the wall says, 'Dr Bill Smith Dental Practitioner'. A curly-headed youth answers the doorbell.

'I'm looking for the dentist. Is he in?' I say.

The youth is the dentist. He looks like he ought to be in secondary school. Maybe he was one of those child geniuses who went to university at fourteen. Professional courtesy prevents me checking the qualification certificates that adorn the walls to make sure they are his.

I lie on the dental chair and he asks what the emergency is. He dons a gown and a surgical mask. He starts tapping at my teeth with his metal chopsticks, like he's expecting to hear musical notes. I explain that I have toothache somewhere, but I'm unsure of the exact location. He flicks on a stereo and Springsteen's 'Born to Run' comes blasting out of several speakers. The kid dentist sings along. His Jack Nicholson eyebrows dance in time to the music. He tells me that I need four fillings and he'll do two today and two next week. Then he gives me the needle.

The needle isn't as painful as I had expected. He doesn't see the need to wait for the Novocain to kick in. He sticks a sucking tube into my mouth and starts fooling around with the drill. He revs it up like he is some boy racer with a souped-up Golf GTI. *Whir, whir.*

I shut my eyes and the drill goes in. Oh, man, the pain. The guy may look like Macaulay Culkin but he drills teeth like he's Laurence Olivier. I'd like to bite the fucker's fingers, but he'd probably drill through my gums.

He stops singing but the eyebrows continue to dance.

This is not worth it, I say to myself. The pain is suffocating. I need to get out of here. I could just quit that job. It's a shit job anyway. Trouble is, getting another shit job may be a problem.

'*Is it safe?*' I imagine the dentist asking.

Fuck you, it's not safe.

I grip the armrests.

'Wider,' he says.

I pray to God in heaven for an end to this torture. The kid dentist looks at me from behind his mask. He shakes his head in pity. He thinks that *I'm* pathetic. He drills some more. *Whir, whir.* The vacuum tube sucks up blood and debris.

'It's been a while, hasn't it?' His eyes close as he grins. 'Will you look at that!' he says.

Springsteen sings another song—for a change, it's about cars, girls and summer in New Jersey. I ask myself how the fuck it has come to this. How did it come to this? How the fuck have I ended up here with psycho teenage-mutant dentist drilling holes in my mouth? If I could trace back over my life, from the beginning, scene by scene, could I find a defining moment where I could say, *'Yes, right there—that was the moment when my slow descent began.'*?

The dentist raises a leg from behind his gown and tries to force one foot onto my lap. 'Try to relax,' he says.

I can't take any more. It's too much. Fuck it! No job is worth this. I shout, 'Stop, Stop!'

He retreats a little, drill in one hand and the sucking tube in the other. He looks like he is posing for a photograph for *Dentist's Digest*. His big eyes give me that hurt puppy-dog look.

My tongue searches my mouth for damage. 'No more, Jesus. No more!' I wipe my mouth with my shirt sleeve, push him aside and stagger for the door. He pulls his mask off and the drill stops whirring.

In the 7-Eleven on Dominic Street, I purchase Solpadeine, toilet roll, soda water and a pack of Gitanes. I flag down a taxi. *Never get out of the boat. Absolutely goddamn right!*

Back at work, I lurk outside Nurse Ratched's office, holding toilet paper to my mouth and clutching, under my arm, the audit files of a radiator manufacturing company from Cloyne. She summons me inside. Her office is even smaller than mine. She sits behind her self-assembled Formica desk, her fingers stroking her telephone. I study the grease spot on the wall where the back of her head has drawn a dark cloud. Rumour around the office is that she has a dragon tattoo on the small of her back. Jimmy Brazil swears that he has seen it. I open my mouth wide and display my frozen chin. Then, just for her, I spit a little blood onto the toilet paper. Both of us are unsure of what to say next.

'Well? How are you feeling now?' she gambits.

I shrug and groan in response.

'Dr Schmidt?' she says.

I explain Dr Schmidt is really Dentist Smith and sometimes he embellishes his credentials. She studies me with her pencil pressed to her lips. I tell her about the ordeal in the dentist's office but I sound like Sam Kinison. I act out the role until I realise that she doesn't understand a word I'm saying. All the while, her fingers never stray far from that phone. I wipe spittle off my chin.

'Mr Rattigan has been enquiring about you.'

Her pencil is back pressed to her lips. She offers no further explanation. Words won't come to me. We stare at each other. They'll make her partner soon, unless she gets pregnant first. Nothing depresses me more than other people's success, except perhaps a friend's success. Luckily for me, I don't have any successful friends.

Nurse Ratched makes a face that is both pained and quizzical. 'You didn't do that to yourself, did you?' she asks.

I swallow a mouthful of gunk and my voice becomes suddenly clear.

'No, no, no—it was the dentist. I don't know what he was trying to do to me.'

She has never been to university. She joined Rattigan, Palmer and Hodge straight out of school. Yet, she is now a qualified accountant and a fellow of the Association. That's better than being a 'made man' in the mafia. She is like Paul Sorvino to my Ray Liotta. I pat blood from my chin and show her the evidence dotted on the tissue paper.

'Does it hurt?'

'It hurts bad.'

'Can I take it that your dental treatment is complete?'

'Definitely,' I say and swallow more blood.

'There will be no more sickies, understand? If you have pneumonia or if some unlucky accident should befall you, then you either come in anyway or don't bother coming back to work here again, understand?'

'I understand.'

She takes her fingers from her phone, and uses her pencil to point to the door.

Later Una sneaks a coffee from the kitchen for me. It dribbles down the frozen side of my face. It doesn't smell of anything like victory. I resolve to balance that farmer's twenty-two bank accounts.

Because of interfering Nurse Ratched, I have to conduct a night-time excursion to the cinema. I never, ever, ever go to the cinema at night, but it's my last chance to see this film. There's a queue at the Kino for cinema tickets, a queue for the toilet and another one for the snack shop. Everywhere I look, there is a queue. I'm early—but I'm still late.

Two noisy lovebirds took up position in the bucket seats behind me. Now I ask you, in today's world of free love, interest-free car loans and room-only hotels, is there really a need for bucket seats in a cinema?

Anyway, I sat there in the dark, safe in the knowledge that I was about to see a film that would have neither horses nor Baldwins of any kind. Seven Psychopaths *is written and directed by one of the greatest living playwrights in the English language: Martin McDonagh. Alas, a great playwright does not a great director make. The film features a bucketful of cool actors—Walken, Rockwell, Harrelson, Waits and Stanton, and along for the ride is our own Colin Farrell.*

The film concerns a screenwriter mixed up in a dognapping. What's a dognapping? That's what you call it when someone kidnaps a dog. Only in LA. Just as it says on the tin there are seven psychopaths in this film—one is usually enough for any film but in this tin, you get seven. It is excruciating nonsense. How bad is it? Well, in one scene, Christopher Walken, is supposed to be "dead" on the roadside but is clearly seen inhaling and exhaling. That's how bad it is. It's as if all the energy that should have gone into the script and direction was used up in pursuing the quality actors. Pretentious postmodern crap like this gives pretentious postmodern critics like me a bad name.

I have never watched a more annoying collection of characters since I last saw The Partridge Family *on television. After five minutes, I wanted to go. But walking out of such a small theatre so early is really making a statement, and I felt that there was enough of that going on already.*

I have never been mugged in my life but I believe this is what a mugging feels like. Seven Psychopaths *is an assault on your senses. It is a mercy when the closing credits appear. There is a message to this film, and the message is this: "I am clever. You will be clever too if you like this movie."*

On the bus home to Rathluirc, the film plays over in my mind. The scenes follow their own dream-like sequence. The bus meanders through the city streets, splashing rainwater onto late night pedestrians. Someone has carved their initials into the cushion of the seat beside me and a wino behind me serenades a schoolgirl with a song made famous by The Pogues.

When I alight the bus in Rathluirc I dither between going to The Sugar Sugar Café for a burnt toast sandwich or going for a pint in The Auld Triangle. I decide to anaesthetise myself against the horrors of the day.

Often the best way to overcome many of life's horrors is to write about them. In the bar I order a pint of Murphy's, a small Jameson chaser and a packet of Bacon Fries. Fat Andy's wearing a torn black overcoat and a beanie cap. The beanie cap might actually be a tea cosy. He whispers my order back to himself to help remember. Foxy John sits at the bar counter watching the television. He takes ages to turn to face me and before he can engage me in conversation I find an empty table beneath the dartboard. Fat Andy brings the drinks to me. I swish the whiskey around my mouth and try to gather it around the torn gum. It burns. The Murphy's cools my mouth and I take another deep drink. I know that as soon as I start writing the review, I won't be aware of Fat Andy behind the counter or Foxy John reading the *Echo* and I won't even be able to hear the television. I root out the Silvine memo book and begin the review all over again:

Regular readers of this column will be aware of my penchant for afternoon cinema-going. The afternoon is truly the only time to see a film; the pensioners never distract you with high fives or hellos, there are no youths attempting to mate and sometimes you have the theatre to yourself …

Six

Choosing My Confessions

2012

Player: Alice Woods

Choosing My Confessions

When I look out through the window of The Sugar Sugar Café I see the traffic stalling on Main Street. There are cars, trucks and SUVs backed up, tail to tail, as far down as the church. Shoppers squeeze between the trucks and cars, crossing to the other side of the street.

A big, shiny, cream-coloured bus crawls into view. It's full of Pasadena redneck tourists. They stare at me like I'm some kind of natural history exhibit. I wave; some wave back.

The truckers, sitting high up in their cabs, rev their engines to the last, in frustration at the traffic jam. The windows of the café vibrate. Some truckers toot their horns in anger and one curly-haired driver, who keeps looking over my way, seems to toot his horn just for me.

For some reason I miss my mom and dad. My mom lives in Buffalo, New York state and my dad lives in a veterans' housing centre in Camden County, New Jersey. They went their separate ways years ago. I miss the oddest things, like the wings they make in the Anchor bar and real football, the kind the Bills play, and Lake Erie. I miss the smell of fresh bagels and the whoosh of the subway on Christopher Street, and the free jazz concerts they used to have downtown in Battery Park. Lemme tell you, I definitely miss the tips I used to get working in the front bar in PJ Clarke's on Third Avenue.

I flick my kitchen towel, nailing another bluebottle against the wall. The café front door springs open. *Fring, fring* goes the bell and in steps Vincent with more clumps of toilet paper stuck to his face. He ought to take more time when he's shaving. He's the wrong side of sixty but somewhere in the back of his mind, he imagines he's still an eligible bachelor. He shuffles over to his table like he's wading into the ocean, unsure of his footing and eager to find someplace safe. He takes a seat in his usual place. Table 8.

'Coffee, Alice, please. And go easy on me today.'

He takes out the *Racing Post* and lays it across the table. His gut sticks out in front, like he's wearing a barrel for pants. He immediately becomes engrossed in the gee-gees. I am dismissed. I go and get his coffee.

Burnt Toast comes into the café, his hair standing right up like Ernie from *Sesame Street*. He looks around and sees Vincent. They exchange grunts and he takes his usual place—table 5, by the window. I give him a menu. He studies it. But I already know what he wants: the same thing he wants every time he comes in here—two crispy pieces of bacon, two slices of burnt toast and coffee.

The radio station plays an early Blondie hit and I sway to the disco rhythm.

Fring, fring, the doorbell tinkles again and a tall lady comes in with a copy of the *Vale Star* newspaper stuck under her arm. She is wearing a tight-fitting white T-shirt, denim dungarees and Roman sandals. I recognise her as O'Sullivan the pharmacist, from across the street. One look at her and you know she's the kind of gal that if she sat on a milkshake she could tell you what flavour it was. She sits down at table 3. I give her a menu, pick up the dead bluebottle by its legs from the linoleum floor and pop it in the trash can.

'You're an American?' Dungaree Lady says to me, like she ought to be in Mensa.

'Uh-huh, that's right, hon. I'm an American, born and bred, though I'm not what you might call a Native American.'

'I have a friend working in New York,' she says.

'Me too,' I say as I wipe down a tabletop.

I put a cup in front of Vincent and start to fill it with

116

coffee from the steel jug. I pour real slow. I watch him pretend to be engrossed in some article about a jockey under investigation for throwing a race. I change tack and start to hold the jug up high, as high as I can, so that the coffee makes the most noise possible as it sloshes down into his cup. Drops of coffee fall onto his newspaper. He looks up from it, not at me but straight ahead. I keep pouring until he says, 'That will do, thanks, Alice.'

Burnt Toast starts writing in his notebook again and I slide over there to see if I can get a peek at what he's writing. He looks up at me.

'What can I get ya hon?'

'The usual, please.'

'What's the usual today?' I smile.

'May I have two slices of toast, burnt through and through, with two crispy rashers and a pot of coffee, please?' He says all formal.

'Sure can, darlin',' I say, making him blush.

Carl is in the alley having a cigarette. I slap the cowbell to get his attention. I snap Burnt Toast's order on the nail block.

Dungaree Lady beckons for me. She points at something near the top of the menu, like maybe I need help with my English. As she speaks, her finger traces the printed words. She wants poached eggs on toast. She also wants hollandaise sauce on the side.

Now, even before I ask him, I know that Carl has no intention of making hollandaise sauce for any customer of The Sugar Sugar Café. We've been down this road before. When Carl is cooking, I find it's best to keep things simple, so I tell the customers we only have what is printed on the menu, and any digressions will not be tolerated by the kitchen staff under any circumstances. It's best to cut things off at the pass when Carl's in the kitchen.

So I explain to Dungaree Lady the situation and she's nodding her head in sympathy, like she understands every single problem I've ever had in my whole miserable life. When it sinks in that she won't be getting her hollandaise, she stops nodding her head. She pulls the menu sharply away and begins to study it all over again. She decides she still wants poached eggs on toast, even without the hollandaise but wants mayonnaise instead. Well, it's been a morning full of crazies and one more won't make much difference. I write up her order and sashay over to the hatch, in time to the music on the radio. Carl is chopping parsley with a meat cleaver.

'I see Vincent the lover boy is in today,' says Carl.

'He is. And he's not my lover boy.'

'Don't know what you see in that guy.'

'I'm so over that guy.'

'Right … right …'

I bang the order on the nail for him and pour myself half a cup of coffee and stare out the window again.

'Alice, Alice, oh Alice, earth calling Alice.' Carl slaps the cowbell and I go get Burnt Toast his breakfast. Carl is wearing this white US naval officer's hat he bought on eBay. He has on a Dire Straits T-shirt that reads 'Brothers in Arms' across the chest.

Burnt Toast says thanks to the plate I lay before him, but not to me. He's busy writing. I watch the traffic again.

Vincent wants more coffee, and I empty the metal pot down the sink and fill the percolator machine again with some good old Robert Roberts. We used to serve only instant Nescafé, but now The Sugar Sugar Café is trying for something more upmarket.

Carl slaps the cowbell, and I go collect the poached eggs. I stare at them, wobbling like little yellow marbles around a piece of sliced toast.

'Hon, that's boiled eggs on toast.'

Carl's hands are a mass of burn scars. He appears puzzled by my comment.

'No, Alice, it's poached eggs on toast.'

'I'm sorry, hon, but those eggs are boiled and I'm not giving that shit to any paying customer.'

'Suit yourself, Alice.'

'Suit yourself? Suit yourself! What's the matter with you? She knows what poached eggs are supposed to look like. She wanted hollandaise—uh-huh, yeah? But I told her how you feel about hollandaise and she still wanted the eggs. Now make some damn poached eggs.'

Carl bins the plate and I wait at the hatch until he starts to poach some new eggs. He looks at me, like somehow I've hurt his feelings.

Burnt Toast has finished his breakfast and wants to pay. He waves a ten euro note about. Carl slaps the cowbell and I go pick up the plate of poached eggs. It's an improvement, but they still don't look like anything I'd want to eat. I pop them in front of Dungaree Lady.

She gives a little sniff and announces to the world, 'I'm not eating this, and I'm not paying for it either.'

'Can you keep your voice down, ma'am?'

'Don't you dare tell me to keep my voice down.'

Lemme tell you that there's nothing I hate more than a bitchin' woman, except maybe for a skinny bitchin' woman. Vincent is smiling to himself as he pretends to read his newspaper. I realise now that he knows Dungaree Lady. Perhaps, even in the biblical sense. I turn up the volume on the radio.

'These eggs are horrible; take the plate away,' Dungaree Lady says.

'Sorry 'bout that, ma'am.'

'I mean, just horrible.'

'I'm sorry about that, ma'am. Can I get you something else?'

'You want me to eat something else?' she says.

'Yes, ma'am, something else. Can I get you something else?'

'You want to get me something else? That would be

like me asking for extra poison!' Dungaree Lady shakes her head.

She and Vincent exchange glances and I get the feeling she's about to cry. She gets up from her chair and walks out the door. The Angelus bells sound off twelve noon. I have never gotten used to those bells; it's like a funeral march.

***

It was Bridie who found Mattie's note on the kitchen table, beneath an eight-ounce can of Batchelors baked beans. I was still in my dressing gown. Bridie held the note in front of my nose like she was returning a bounced cheque.

'Mattie has left you,' she said. 'He's finally left you, high and dry. Not for another woman, mind you. He's left you and your child, so as to make a fresh start for himself. Mattie's gone.'

She left the note fall from her fingers. It twirled like a leaf and seemed to take forever to reach the floor. Bridie leaned back against the door and lit a cigarette.

I got down on my knees to read the note. Bridie turned down the volume on the radio in case it interfered with the show.

Dear Alice, the letter began and I knew right then she wasn't lying. *There is something I have to say to you …*

Mattie never gave a proper reason, just said he had to go. He never said where he was going. Never mentioned Billy. He signed off with an *x*. The note was mercifully short.

I read his childish scrawl, over and over again. Each time I read it, it seemed to hurt me more. Bridie made her sucking noises with her false teeth as she prepared to speak and I stumbled for the back door. My head in a spin, I sat on the stoop. I could hardly breathe.

I found Billy in Ollie's shed. He was sitting on the concrete floor, watching the clothes in the washing machine go round and round. I called, but he didn't hear me.

The doctors over here say Billy has autism spectrum disorder, back in New York the doctors said he has ADHD. The doctors put labels on people like it's gonna help; it doesn't help. My mom puts labels on her pickle jars but it doesn't manage to describe the contents either.

I called louder but he didn't hear me. I screamed at him. Then I made the mistake of looking back towards the

123

house and I could see Bridie and Ollie watching me through the window. Bridie smiled smugly like she'd nailed a full house on Telebingo.

I screamed at Billy as loud as I could but he still acted like he was stone deaf. I walked towards him and touched his face and then he smiled up at me.

I brought him down to The Auld Triangle on Main Street. I drank a sea breeze and Billy ate salt and vinegar potato chips, his favourite.

'Look, Billy, I brought you here to tell you something. There's no easy way to tell you this so I'm just going to say it, straight out … your father has walked out on us. I don't know where he's gone. He's just gone.'

'When will Dad be back?'

'He's not coming back, sweetie.'

'Not ever?'

'I don't know. I guess not ever.'

'Where has Dad gone?'

I buried my face behind my hands. I felt numb but I knew I had to keep it together for Billy's sake. 'Dad feels the need to live by himself awhile so I don't know where he's gone, sweetie, I don't know.'

'Do Nana and Granddad know where Dad is gone?'

'Well no, sweetie, they don't. They're real cut up about it too. Just as much as me and you.'

I ate some of his potato chips.

'Will Dad be back at the weekend?'

'No, sweetie, he won't. He's not ever coming back.'

'It's because of me, isn't it? It's my fault Dad's gone. I bet it's because of me,' he said.

'No, no, no, sweetie, that's so not true. Your dad wants to see more of the world one more time. That's all.'

'Who will take care of us now?' he said.

'Aw, baby, we'll take care of each other, won't we? Aren't we the two very best friends? Aren't we?'

'I guess,' he said.

'For sure, the two best friends ever and we'll always stick together, just like always.'

'We'll have to go now?' he said.

'We'll go home soon, in a minute. Mommy needs another drink first.'

'No, I mean, where will we live now?'

'What do you mean, sweetie?'

'They won't want us, not Nana and Granddad,' he said.

'Oh! Oh! don't you worry. I'll find us a place, sweetie. A place with hot water and a shower. We'll be able to do whatever we want. We can even get us a dog. Just the two of us.'

'And Dad too,' he said.

'I don't think so, sweetie.'

'I don't want to live with Nana and Granddad anymore.'

'Me neither, sweetie, me neither.'

Mattie had emptied our savings account in the credit union—28,000 euro. That was meant to be a deposit on a new house in Wiltshire Lawns. I could have called the police, but I didn't. Looking back, I feel it made me even stronger.

Only God and Bridie know where Mattie is now, and God's keepin' shtum. Mattie may even be back in New York, sweet-talking another broad. I don't care anymore.

Bridie and Ollie never asked us to pack our bags but every time I entered the house the conversation went dead.

Carl offered us a room in his flat. I've seen his flat; as much as I wanted to escape Bridie's phoney piety I couldn't have Billy living in a cold-water bachelor flat on Clancy Terrace with posters of Bo Derek on the wall.

Every day for weeks I phoned Mom in Buffalo. I told her she had been right all along. Everything she had to say about the Irish was true. They couldn't be trusted. Everything she said about Mattie was right. He couldn't be trusted the most. I cried on the phone to her. I cried like a little girl. This seemed to cheer her up no end.

'I told ya, didn't I tell ya? But ya wouldn't listen, would ya? No. Ya never listen to your own mother. That's always been your problem.'

'I still love him, Mom, I love him to bits.'

'Jesus Christ, lady, will ya listen to yourself …'

I could hear her light up one of her Luckies. When she's on the phone Mom always reaches for her Luckies.

'Ya need to come home, Alice. Forget Ireland, forget New York. Come back to Buffalo. Find a place to live. Somewhere close by my apartment. Get a job. I'd love to have you and Billy live with me but I got my arthritis now … so you know …'

127

'I know that, Mom.'

'If there was somebody over there that could take care of Billy, huh? Billy's grandparents maybe, the Irish ones? You could come live with me a while, if it was just you. There's enough room here for two.'

'I can't do that, Mom. I'm not leaving Billy. Are you crazy?'

'Alice, you need to take care of yourself. You need to start doing for Alice now.'

'I can't, Mom. I can't leave Billy.'

Mattie is a slimeball jerk off but he was right about one thing: over here is the best place for Billy. That much was true.

Jerry helped us find the house in Deerpark Heights, a semi-detached house with a back garden. A friend of his was looking for a reliable tenant.

'Well, hell, that's us,' I said.

***

Soon enough, everybody has left the café, except for me and Vincent. I watch him study the ponies. Rubbing his chin. Sticking his bookie's midget pen into his ear and giving it a good scratch. Vincent has broad shoulders and most of his own teeth and big, brown, soulful eyes. I guess if he ever gets around to getting a decent haircut, buying a smart suit and has a proper shave, he might someday be called handsome. Lemme tell you though, that'd be a stretch for 'handsome', so it would.

A song comes on the radio. A song about choosing confessions and I stand still and listen. It's like they're playing that song just for me.

Carl is refusing to talk to me. He's banging pots around in the kitchen like he's suffering premenstrual tension. When I was growing up Mom used to warn me about men and the trouble they would bring but she never warned me of the trouble I would bring upon myself.

I step out onto the street and light up a Marlboro. I use a Dixie cup to catch the fallen ash and I stare at the traffic struggling to get through Main Street.

Seven

Billy Frankenstein

2012

Player: Billy Woods

Billy Frankenstein

Mom tries to kiss me on the forehead. I duck out of her reach. She yanks at the straps of my school satchel. I pull away and run through the school gates, into the yard. She calls after me, 'Billy, Billy, sweetie, give your mommy a kiss.' All the boys in the schoolyard stop whatever it is they're doing and stare at this big, fat, crazy American woman, shouting through the railings to her son, 'Mommy loves you, Billy.' I keep running. I crash into another boy, knocking him to the ground. He's a bigger boy, from the high school boy next door—Colin Roche. He curses me and Mom shouts, 'Be careful, baby'. I cover my ears with my hands as I run. I scream the words of my favourite Marilyn Manson song, 'Rock 'n' Roll Nigger'. I don't look back: I know what she looks like.

I hang my bomber jacket from a hook in the locker room and slip inside my favourite stall, the only one with the working latch. I put my satchel over the toilet bowl and sit on it. There's a box of matches in my satchel. When I try lighting them they're too damp. Someone uses the stall next to mine to make a piss. I cover my ears and sing another Marilyn Manson song to myself, 'This is the New Shit', and wait for the bell to tell me it's time for class.

The boys at school call me 'Billy Frankenstein'. They think it's funny. Even the smaller kids call me Billy Frankenstein. They're not afraid of me. They should be afraid: everyone should be afraid. Someday my dad is gonna come back to Ireland for me and we're gonna do stuff together. Nobody will be able to stop us doing what we want. Not my mom or my granddad or Nana—just no one—because he's my only dad, and I'm his only son.

The bell rings. I hate that bell. I hate that bell so much that I can't even tell you how much I hate that bell. I don't see why it has to be so loud. The best bell—the only bell I like—is the three o'clock bell. That's the going-home-time bell. That's the bell that tells everybody's mom that we have to go now. But that bell will not ring for a long, long time. That's the furthest away bell.

I sit beside 'Polish Pawel'. He's a dork. He's not my friend. Polish Pawel is nobody's friend, not even mine. He thinks I'm dumb just because I come from New York, like that was the test and I passed that test for sure. Well, he's from Poland; whatever that says about him, I don't know. I'm not dumb. I'm way smart for my age. My mom tells me all the time how smart I am. Polish Pawel is the dumb one.

Miss Hurley is teacher's name. She's very pretty.

'Right, boys, get the homework out,' she says.

Polish Pawel kicks my ankle.

'Miss, Miss, Miss, I don't have my homework done,' I say.

'Why's that, Billy?'

'I couldn't do it, Miss.'

'Okay, Billy, thank you. Now the rest of you, get your homework out of your bags, please.'

Miss Hurley writes some Gaelic words on the chalk board. I don't understand Gaelic. Polish Pawel doesn't understand Gaelic either. We make faces at each other all the time during Gaelic. We try to make each other laugh. The Gaelic words are so hard. Polish Pawel says that the words on the chalk board are really Polish cuss words. He tells me what the words really mean. I laugh. I can't help myself.

Miss Hurley sees me laughing. She asks me something in Gaelic. I can't answer. I don't understand one word of what she's saying. Everybody else laughs at me, including Polish Pawel. Miss Hurley comes closer to me. She stands over me, talking in Gaelic. She wags a finger at me and then at Polish Pawel. Everybody's laughing. I don't understand why I have to learn a whole new language when the only person in the world who speaks the language is Miss Hurley. It's not fair. The bell rings for 'little break.' Miss Hurley gathers her books. She gives me a dirty look. Polish Pawel says something gross about her as she leaves the classroom.

At break, I stand beside Polish Pawel in the yard. The rest of the boys play soccer in the field.

After break Miss Hurley takes a globe from the shelf and places it on her desk. The globe is made of tin and is the size of a beach ball.

I raise my hand. She can't see that my hand is up. I shake my hand about. When I get tired, I swop hands and shake the other one.

'Miss, Miss, Miss,' I say. She can't hear me.

'Miss, the Earth is forever expanding,' I say.

Miss Hurley still can't hear me.

She unfolds a map of Europe and pins it to the whiteboard.

'Miss, did you know scientists have proved the Earth keeps expanding?' I say.

Later I notice that the classroom clock is telling the wrong time again. The clock tells me that it is 12.38 p.m., but my Spiderman watch tells me that it is 12.45 p.m.— lunchtime already. That's what they do over here all the time, whenever they feel like it: they change the clocks.

They turn them back when they want you to sit in class for longer, and they turn them forward when they want you back from lunch break sooner.

'Miss, Miss, Miss, the clock is wrong again.' I use one hand to hold the other hand up so she can see I have a question.

'The clock's fine, Billy.'

'It's wrong, Miss.'

'It's fine.'

'No, Miss, it's gone wrong again.'

'Put your hand down, Billy.'

'I've no homework done, Miss.'

'I know, Billy, you told me.'

After school, I sit a while in the same stall and I wait until I know for sure that Mom'll be at the school gate.

'What did you learn today?' she says.

'Nothing. Can we go to the park?'

'No, Billy, I want to go home and take a nap before I go back to work.'

'Please, Mom, please, please.'

'Billy, your mom's feet hurt so much.'

'I'll be good for Mrs Roche tonight, honest I will.'

'No,' she says.

'I'll be good all weekend, honest. No tantrums, not

even a little one. I promise. I'll go to bed early. I'll even tidy my room—please, Mom, please.'

I stop walking beside her. My schoolbag slips out of my hand and falls to the ground. I stare at the footpath. She looks down at me.

'Come on, Billy, let's go home.'

I make out like I'm a statue.

'Billy, please, if you knew how tired Mommy is, you'd come on home.'

She pulls my school sweater.

Statues don't move.

'Okay, Billy. We'll go to the park. But I'm just gonna sit okay, read my magazine. I'm not doing anything. I'm not pushing you on the carousel or racing you on the swings. Mommy's dead beat, alright?'

'Jesus Christ, Mom, I'm not five.'

She sits on a bench. Takes her shoes off. Starts to pick her toes. She talks to this other guy on the other end of the bench. She seems to know him. Maybe she wants to go on a date with him. He has stupid looking hair that stands up in the front.

I climb the rope steps to the pirate ship. I twirl the steering wheel. Ahoy, ahoy. Someone has carved the words 'Fuck You' into the seat of the pirate ship. The metal slide is hot and shiny. I dive down head first and land on the rubber floor. Another mom with a buggy watches me.

I climb back up again and slide down. My mom lights up a cigarette. I sit on the swing and push myself high into the air. Higher and higher. The swing goes *whoosh* and I scream out 'Woo hoo!'. My stomach tingles like I have feathers inside. Leaning back on the swing as far as I can, I let my hair touch the wood chippings on the ground as I rush forward.

'Don't do that, Billy,' Mom calls, in that calm tone of voice she uses sometimes.

It's the voice she uses when she wants to threaten me but without making other people aware she's threatening me.

'Billy, sweetie, don't dirty your hair like that,' she says.

I hate that voice so much. She's pretending to be sweet for strangers.

'Woo hoo!'

She stands up.

'Race me, Mom.'

'No.'

'Race me, Mom, please.'

'I'm not gonna race you, Billy. I'm too tired, so

forget it.'

She says something to another mom. I can't hear.

'Please, Mom, just once and I won't ask you anymore.'

'Nope, told you already, I'm too damn tired,' she says.

'Please, Mom, please.'

'No.'

'Please, please, please.'

I sit on the carousel. It spins around in a circle. I stand up on the carousel and try to moonwalk.

'You're gonna fall and break your neck,' she says.

I try walking faster on the carousel. I slip and fall off.

'Tole ya, sweetie—next time you'll break your neck,' she says.

'It'll be your fault,' I say.

'No, it won't,' she says.

'Will you push me on the carousel, Mom, please? I won't fall off if you push me.'

'Billy, will you give me some peace? Please, I'm begging ya.'

Maybe the other mom with the buggy will push me or maybe the guy sitting next to Mom will push me?

They're staring at me. I'm afraid to ask them.

'Why won't you push me, Mom?'

'Because I'm tired, sweetie. Because my energy is gone. I'm running on empty. Got just enough to keep going and no more than that.'

'Push me, Mom, push me, Mom.'

The other mom with the buggy keeps stares at me. I make a zombie face at her. Fuck her.

Mom takes a magazine out of her bag and starts reading it. I get off the carousel and climb the metal rope tent all the way to the very top. I can see forever up there. I can see the church and the school and the purple hills to the south. Mom wants me down. She's standing now. She has her magazine all rolled up, like a bat. She thinks she can swat me from all the way down there.

'Billy, you're way too high.'

I hold my hand above my eyes like a pirate when he looks out to sea.

'Billy, honey, Mommy wants you down, now.'

There's that voice of hers again. The most annoying thing in the whole wide world. I get another idea. I stick my legs through the highest rung on the rope tent and hang my body upside down. My hair falls south and I can feel my brain filling up with blood. A gummy bear falls out of my school pants pocket and down to the ground.

'Don't do this, Billy. Please, baby, come down,' she says.

I was saving that damn gummy bear: now I'll never find it among the wood chippings.

'Jesus, Billy, you get down here, pronto. You could fall and kill yourself. Do ya hear me, mister? Don't make me climb up there. Lemme tell you something, Mommy's sure gonna kick your ass when she catches hold of ya.'

She's walking around the base of the rope tent, squawking like it's on fire or something. She starts beating on my school satchel with her magazine—like that's gonna hurt me. I close my eyes and fold my arms across my chest, like I am praying to God upside down. Every drop of blood in my body must have landed in my head by now.

'I'm coming to get ya,' She shouts. 'I'm gonna climb up this fucking thing and get ya, and when I get ya, I'm gonna fucking throw you off the top. Then we'll see who thinks this is funny.'

I open one eye. She has her shoes off and she's trying to raise a leg onto the bottom rung of the tent. She looks like one of those WWF wrestlers climbing through the ropes around the ring. She manages to get one leg up onto the bottom rung. The rope tent shudders. My body swings to the side. I feel woozy. Mom hops up and down with one leg on the lower rung and one on the ground.

'Fuck you, Billy, you little turd,' she shouts up at me.

I almost slip off. I grip the ropes tighter. Brussels is the capital city of Belgium. Mom succeeds in getting both legs onto the first level. She bounces up and down, like she's on a trampoline. I start bouncing up and down, like I'm on a trampoline.

'Mom, Mom, it's okay, I'm getting down—I'm getting down!'

'You betcha,' she says.

'No, Mom, I promise I'm coming down. Please don't climb up any higher, it's too dangerous.' Brussels is not in France though a lot of people believe it is.

'Too late now, you little shit.'

'Look up at me, Mom, I'm getting down. See?' I straighten up.

She looks up at me.

'Do ya swear?' she says.

'I swear it, Mom, scout's honour—just don't climb up any more.'

'Alright then, Billy, I'm getting off,' she says.

'Mom? Mom? Stop. Please, Mom, can you get off

slowly?'

She sits on the bench again, trying to light up a cigarette but her breathing's not right yet. The other mom with the buggy is gone. I climb down. Mom spreads out along the bench like she's slowly melting. She reads her magazine. A boy plays soccer with his dad. The dad can kick the ball so high into the air that it could get lost in the clouds. I run towards the dad. The boy's younger than me. He's not in my school.

'Can I play with you guys?'

The dad says okay but the boy says nothing. We form a triangle and kick the ball to each other. I kick the ball as high into the air as I possibly can and the dad tries to catch it. The boy kicks the ball to me but he can't kick it as high as me. I look over at Mom. She puffs her cigarette and waves to me. She can see how high I can make the ball go. The boy gives up. He stands with his head bent down, staring at the grass. So it's just the dad and me. I bet the dad wishes his son was more like me.

'Come on, Billy, we gotta go,' Mom shouts to me.

'Soon, okay?'

'We're going now, Billy, okay?' she says.

The dad holds the football in his hands like it's a prize.

'Billy, come on now, sweetie.'

I motion to the dad to kick the ball.

'Billy, we need to go,' she says.

The dad doesn't kick the ball.

'Come on,' I say to the dad but he won't kick the ball.

'Billy, please come on home,' she says.

'Whatever,' I say.

I don't know why she has to do this. Whenever I start having a good time she always has to come and spoil everything. She's always interfering with my life.

The boy pulls at his dad's sweater, and his dad bends to the boy's height. The boy whispers something in his ear.

'Keep the fucking ball!' I say to the dad.

'Billy! I said now, mister,' Mom says. She marches towards me. She catches hold of my arm. She pulls hard. They speak French and Dutch in Belgium.

I try to hold still. She pulls harder. The little boy stands close to his dad.

'Sorry,' Mom says to the dad.

The boy watches me and Mom walking away.

***

Mom makes dinner: chicken nuggets, French fries and

peas. I watch the margarine melt over the peas. She steals one of my French fries. I wish she'd steal the peas. After dinner I have to do my homework. I'm not allowed watch tv until my homework is done and she has corrected it. She always finds stupid mistakes in my homework. She is kind of good at Math but she's no good at English; she can't spell for shit. Homework sucks and takes forever. It is so stupid to have lots of homework.

Mrs Roche comes over at 6 p.m. She acts kind of posh for a babysitter, but she's not posh. Mom calls her a 'stuck-up bitch'. I'm not allowed to call her a bitch. I am allowed to call her a witch—I can get away with that. Mrs Roche brings her son, Colin, with her. He's in the school next to mine. He's older than me. He has a basketball.

Mom corners me in the hallway and forces a kiss on me. Nobody sees her kiss me. She warns me to be good for Mrs Roche. I tell her that I'll be good if she brings me home a lollipop. My favourite lollipop in the whole wide world is orange-flavoured Chupa Chups. She promises to leave one under my pillow if I'm good for Mrs Roche.

From my bedroom window, I watch Mom get into the car in the street below. This is always a big operation for Mom, getting in and getting out of her car. I'm hoping that she never gets the car to start. She sets the hazard lights flashing and then the wipers start flapping and the car disappears down the road.

I look out at the neighbours' houses. Some have their lights on. Some have fires lit. Some kids on bikes cycle down our street. They look up at me and I wave but they don't wave back.

Later, I hear Mrs Roche's son playing ball in our yard. I watch him from the bathroom window. I can hear the theme song to *Coronation Street*.

She calls to me, 'Billy, come down and play ball with our Colin.'

I pretend I don't hear her.

'Get down here now or I'll be having a word with your mam later on.'

I go outside to the backyard and sit on top of the yellow gas bottle.

'Wanna shoot some hoops?' Colin says.

'We don't have hoops.'

'She watching *Coronation Street*?' he says.

'Uh-huh.'

We throw the basketball against the wall, as though there was a net there. Colin can't dribble the ball, but he can catch it good enough. He jumps against me. His zip on his jacket scrapes against my face as he jumps. He can jump higher than me. He rubs his fingers through my hair. I push his hand away. He tries to spin the ball on one finger. His teeth are crooked and stick out everywhere and when he smiles, it looks like they are all rushing to get out of his mouth.

'What's in there?' he says, pointing to the boiler house.

'Nothing.'

He goes inside. He calls out through the gaps in the boiler house door, 'Billy Frankenstein, Billy Frankenstein! Come here, Billy Frankenstein!'

'Shut up.' I say.

He won't let up using his stupid cartoon voices.

I kick the basketball down to the end of the yard. Suddenly he opens the door. His pants and shorts are in a bundle on the floor. He grabs hold of my sweater and pulls me inside the shed. I try to push him away. He catches hold of my hair and pulls my head, down to the ground. The side of my head smacks against the concrete floor. He kneels up on top of my back. I can't move. I can't breathe. He pulls at my jeans.

'You'll enjoy this, young Billy,' he says.

I try to twist away from him. He grunts and laughs. He starts to whack himself off while sitting on top of me. I can taste the dust and grit on the boiler house floor. He makes animal noises. Somehow I manage to pull my knees up, and he falls off me and crashes into the boiler. I run out of the shed. Belgium is where they make the most chocolate.

Mrs Roche is annoyed that I have come back inside the house. She holds a chocolate cookie in her hand. She dunks it slowly into her tea.

'Billy? Where're you going? Where's our Colin?'

I climb the stairs. It takes forever to find my iPod. I tear up my bedroom looking for it. Throwing away every useless thing that gets in my way.

Mom says my brain works different to other people. She says for most people, solving a problem is like solving a jigsaw puzzle but for me, it's like putting together pieces from different puzzles.

The iPod is stuffed inside my Converse sneaker. Mom's room is open. I lie down on her bed and bury my head beneath a pillow. I smell all those woman smells: perfumes, powders and soaps. I dial up my iPod, full blast, then close my eyes. Marilyn Manson: I know all the words to 'Personal Jesus'.

Later my mom wakes me when she gets home from work at The Sugar Sugar Café. She has a Chupa Chups lollipop for me, cherry-cola flavour. She takes the wrapper off and holds the lollipop up to my nose. I keep my eyes closed because if she knows I'm awake, she'll make me go to my own room.

'How are ya doin', sweetie? Did you get on alright with the old bat?'

Mom's trying to trick me into answering her but I don't answer. She flicks on the TV and sits on the end of the bed. She undresses. I squeeze my eyes tighter. I don't want to see her in her underwear. She goes and takes a shower and I open my eyes and stare at the lollipop lying on the pillow next to me. I take the lollipop and hide under the duvet. Then Mom gets into bed beside me. She's wearing the striped pyjamas my dad left behind when he took off and, for once, she lets me sleep all through the night in their bed.

Eight

The Auld Triangle

A story from the past

Player: Jerry Doyle

The Auld Triangle

The last time I was on a batter, was in August 1979 when I was on a two-day drinking spree with my friend Joey O'Keefe. Joey liked to drink Hennessy brandy, when he could afford it; otherwise, he drank Bulmers in summer and Guinness in winter. I liked lager myself, winter or summer. I drank any kind of lager—Harp, Carling, Fürstenberg— they all tasted the same to me. And when I was full to the brim with lager, I liked gin and tonics. The seasons didn't matter so much to me. Joey called me a philistine when it came to drink but it wasn't the drink I liked, so much as the alcohol.

My father had been a corporal in the British Army and served in India. In the short time we lived together in the same house, him and me never stopped arguing. He died of pancreatic cancer in the Regional Hospital in Cork at the start of that summer in 1979 and, instead of grieving, I was mightily relieved. People were forever sympathising with me, shaking my hand, and I did appreciate that. They'd ask me if I missed my father and I'd answer truthfully and say 'not really'. But I did miss the sympathy when that finally petered out.

Anyway, back to that night in August 1979. Joey

and me were having a drink in The Auld Triangle. We were playing a game of 'forty-five' with Fat Andy the pub owner, and some cattle dealer from Meelin. The cattle dealer wore sideburns that ran down to his chin that made him a ringer for one of the Wolfe Tones.

Fat Andy kept the score of the card game on the back of a flattened box of Sweet Afton. Every few minutes we paused playing cards to gaze at the Dublin Horse Show on the black and white telly. The Irish team wore stiff dark coloured uniforms and sat on their horses, expressionless. Some of them were army officers. The sound on the telly was low but you could still hear the plummy voice of the commentator. It was 'clare rind' for 'clear round'.

'The Irish are favourites to win the Aga Khan Trophy this year,' said the cattle dealer.

'Is tha' right, cove?' said Joey.

'Indeed then it is—Eddie Macken is going well, going very well,' said the cattle dealer and added slowly, '… on Boomerang.'

He said the horse's name like this was the nugget of information we had all been waiting to hear.

'Tha' right?' said Joey.

The cattle dealer's hands were the size of shovels; his nails were black and bitten into submission. This was a disadvantage when it was time to pick his nose, which was another habit he clearly enjoyed. When he held the cards in his hairy fingers, the cattle dealer mashed the cards out of shape. He knew he was torturing me.

'Another penalty fine for you, Jerry,' said Fat Andy, his voice rasping from somewhere within his huge frame. He spoke through his teeth like he was trying to bite every word. A perpetual cloud of smoke from his Sweet Afton followed him around the bar. He pencilled a circle around my score and deducted another twenty points from me and I tossed another fifty pence coin into the kitty.

The cattle dealer laughed at me; I was fucked again in that particular round of cards.

'Is Harvey Smith still riding Harvester?' Fat Andy turned to the telly.

'No, I believe he's retired now.' The cattle dealer shoved his big pinky finger up his nose and rooted around till he found something.

'Who's retired? Harvey or Harvester?' said Fat Andy.

I tried to look away from the cattle dealer as he examined his catch as though he were an anthropologist. And like a fly drawn to the electric light I could not look away. Carefully he moulded the snot in his thick fingertips until it became a round ball and then with a grin he flicked it across the bar where it landed somewhere in the darkened corner amongst the cobwebs.

I lifted the fresh pint of Harp from the floor and placed it on a Guinness beer mat on the table. Froth spilled down the sides of the glass. I licked it off my fingers and studied the beer bubbles rising to the top like little shooting stars.

'Who's retired?' said the cattle dealer finally. 'That'd be Harvey—he'd be way too heavy now for the horses to be jumping over them high fences, like. Them are fair big fences now.'

The greatest feeling in the world is the time between the third and fourth pint of lager. This is a universal truth. At this point the brain is coherent, while the troubles of this world are somewhat removed. Friends become better friends, jokes become funnier and stories become better told. At this time, the drinker has a foot in both worlds: the inebriated world and the sober world. Above all else, the drinker wants to maintain this state of balance in the universe.

I used to feel a terrible dread when the supply of alcohol became threatened in any way. That would only ever happen in two ways: when last orders were taken, and, worst of all, when I ran out of money. Back then I did some things when I was drinking, the kind of things that I would rather forget now. Sometimes, people come into my café and they give me the 'look', and I know what's going through their minds—the memory of some night, twenty or thirty years ago, when I was drunk and foolish.

'Some of them fences must be twelve feet high, that's a fact,' droned the cattle dealer.

I'd already lost a share of that week's dole money in the card game. And worse again, the cattle dealer from Meelin had the larger part of it. Joey was up a little money and Fat Andy was about breaking even.

The cattle dealer was one of those fellas who could never call a thing by its rightful name. Everything was a euphemism for something else. He called the king of trumps the 'boss monarch'; he called the knave 'Johnny'. The ten of spades was 'the American hearse'. And he never called me 'Jerry'—he called me 'cove' or 'client'. I gulped at my pint; Joey winked at me and I took another long drink of lager.

'Ye'll be heading for the dance soon, I suppose,' said the cattle dealer.

I didn't answer and neither did Joey.

'Who's playing the Hi-Land ballroom tonight?'

154

said Fat Andy.

'Johnny Logan,' said Joey.

'Johnny Logan? Johnny Logan draws a crowd,' said Fat Andy.

'He draws the moths anyway,' said Joey.

'Indeed then he does,' said the cattle dealer to Joey. '…But small boys like you shouldn't be allowed go to dances.'

'Small jockey, big whip,' said Joey.

'Is that right?'

'Yes, that's right and besides, any man can climb a fallen tree.' Joey wiped froth off his mouth.

'Is that right?' said the cattle dealer again.

'Yeah, that's right—and I've a hundred more if you want to hear them,' said Joey.

'I simply asked were ye boys off to the dance?'

'Don't say anything, cove, just play a fucking card,' said Joey.

The cattle dealer pretended to be offended. In truth, Joey was notorious in the dance halls for asking the tallest women for a slow dance.

A trio of middle-aged tourists came into the bar looking for the toilets. Two men and a woman. They were loud, tired and had come from Shannon airport. Fat Andy abandoned the card game and took up position behind the counter. He straightened his lank comb-over and tightened the knot in his tie.

When the tourists came back out of the toilets, they asked for a wine menu. Fat Andy put a bottle of wine on the counter. It was red, it was French and it was called Baron Charles. The tourists passed the bottle around, taking turns to read the label. They called for whiskeys all around instead and tried to pronounce *sláinte* to each other.

The elder of the two men was named Frederic and soon we learned that he was from Johannesburg. He offered to buy us all a drink. Joey ordered a double brandy with a dash of Sandeman port and I called for a double gin and tonic. The cattle dealer ordered a Murphy's.

Fat Andy filled an ice tray with tap water and carried it out the back to the deep freezer he kept in the store among the beer barrels. Joey offered the tourists one of his rollies from his metal box, but only the woman smoked and she preferred her own menthol cigarettes. Her name was Margaret. I offered her a light but failed to catch her eye even as she cusped the flame. She and the men were lecturers from some university in England.

The Auld Triangle was real 'old world', meaning it was dark, dirty, smoky and uncomfortable. However, the visitors seemed in no rush to get to their hotel in Mallow. I wondered would they notice the frayed copy of the 1916 Proclamation encased on the wall or the black-and-white poster of Pádraig Pearse looking up towards the frayed electrical fuse box. Some part of me wanted to draw their attention to the posters, just to see their reaction and maybe to get them to read a little of the Proclamation. Another part of me wanted to join their conversation, like the cattle dealer had done.

I didn't believe there were many bars like The Auld Triangle in England, or Johannesburg for that matter. Having lived in Birmingham I knew the drink measures are bigger there than in Ireland and maybe that's what made the lecturers so mellow. Anyway, mostly I was trying to figure out which of the men was with the woman. The younger fella drank more quickly and gave off the impression that he would rather be at the bar in the hotel lounge than slumming it in The Auld Triangle.

Without being summoned, the cattle dealer belted out 'The Wild Rover'. It could've been worse, I suppose. He could have recited one of his infamous self-penned poems about the solitude of a bachelor farmer's life. I gulped my drink. When it was drained, I took the slice of lemon in my mouth and sucked the flesh from its skin.

Then I went for a piss. I counted my money in the toilet; I'd just enough for the dance, a couple more pints and maybe enough for a spice burger too.

When I got back from the toilet, there was a fresh gin and tonic waiting for me. Frederic had bought another round of drinks. He told Joey and me that he was a lecturer in African languages. He was small and sturdy and when he sucked in air, he never seemed to let it back out again. He spoke like that David Attenborough fella on the nature programmes. He asked us if we spoke Irish and I lied that I spoke it fluently. He wanted to hear something in Irish, so I spoke the first couple of lines from the national anthem. He listened to me with great intent, as though I was saying something profound. Joey let me have my little joke.

Joey addressed Frederic as 'sir'. It was 'sir' this and 'sir' that as if we were in school. I bent my head in shame. Joey made me feel like we were back in the days again, when fellas like me and Joey had to call gentlemen like Frederic 'sir'. At that moment I think I despised Joey. And every time he called Frederic 'sir' I felt a stabbing in my stomach. And I despised Frederic too, for allowing another man to demean himself in such a way, and in truth I despised myself for sitting there listening to them talk, and what was it all for? The price of another drink.

The cattle dealer let out a roar at the telly. I looked up—Eddie Macken was leaning off his horse and doffing his cap to the fans in the stands. Ireland had won the Aga Khan Trophy.

'Go on, ya boyo,' shouted the cattle dealer.

'Well done, Ireland!' said Frederic to Joey and me, like we'd played a part in the Aga Khan victory.

The younger lecturer shuffled his way to the counter and quietly called for another round of drinks. Foxy John came into the bar and sat by the television.

Frederic told Joey and me about South Africa. He said he was a Zulu warrior and we let him believe it, even though he was as white as my arse. I don't know why I did it, but I told Frederic that this was a great coincidence because the cattle dealer—who was busy at the other end of the bar, talking to Margaret and the younger man—was also a Zulu warrior. Frederic snorted but I insisted the cattle dealer was a real Zulu warrior from a long line of Zulu warriors that had immigrated to Ireland sometime after the famine. Frederic eyeballed the cattle dealer, then called to Fat Andy for another round of drinks with instructions not to include the cattle dealer this time. They were on first name terms at this stage: 'Andy' and 'Frederic'.

Frederic called across the bar to the cattle dealer—

something that must have been in Zulu. The cattle dealer looked confused but laughed in response; it seemed the right thing to do. Frederic was not satisfied and said something else in Zulu—this time more urgent in tone. The cattle dealer began to look anxious. He searched the faces of the visitors for clues as to what was happening, but nobody seemed to know. Margaret looked at her watch. Frederic shouted louder in Zulu, challenging the cattle dealer, and this time no translation was necessary. The whole bar went quiet.

'It's outrageous,' Frederic shouted to the bar at large.

Joey and I tried to hide our laughter behind our drinks.

'That man is an outrageous imposter, I tell you,' said Frederic addressing the bar as you might address a courtroom.

'What's outrageous?' said the cattle dealer. 'Why are you saying "outrageous" to me? I'm not outrageous.'

Frederic performed some aggressive dance movements. I got out of his way. It was like the war dance that the All Blacks do before a rugby game. I stood back as he worked his way down along the bar towards the cattle dealer, screaming fiendish, unintelligible words.

'Jesus!' said Joey.

'What's the matter, Frederic?' said Fat Andy.

'Freddy, for God's sake, behave!' said Margaret.

The younger colleague tried to calm Frederic. Frederic shrugged him away and beckoned the cattle dealer to come closer. I know it was cruel of me to laugh at the discomfort of the cattle dealer, but laugh I did. I laughed until my stomach ached and I felt like throwing up.

Frederic stopped his war dance suddenly. He looked quizzically at the cattle dealer. He spoke in a new softer tone. 'Smithy? Smithy? Is it you? Why have you come here, here of all places?'

The cattle dealer said, 'I ... I don't know ...'

Frederic reached out a hand and addressed the cattle dealer in a tender voice. 'I haven't forgotten you, Smithy. How could I ever forget you?'

'Oh, sweet Jesus!' said Joey to me.

Frederic continued. 'Now, here you are, Smithy. I've found you in Eire for goodness' sake. After all these years. I've missed you so much.'

Margaret gathered her cigarettes and bag and stood up. Fat Andy came out from behind the counter with a yard brush he rarely used. Joey drained his brandy and rubbed his hands together.

A driver type appeared from nowhere. He led the visitors to the exit door. Margaret gave me a look that stopped me laughing. Frederic buried his head in his jacket and allowed himself to be ushered outside. There were no goodbyes or cheerios from them. There was no 'See you in Cambridge'.

Fat Andy collected the empties. The cattle dealer watched the dregs fall to the bottom of his pint. Nobody spoke. Joey studied the dirt on his desert boots. Foxy John did his best impression of a pious saint stumbling into a whore house and I looked out the window as the visitors boarded a black taxi.

The ads came on the telly and I walked out the door and headed back to my house for a change of shirt.

Later, I collected Joey outside The Greasy Spoon. He had bought chips and spice burgers. Then I kicked my Honda 50 into life and Joey climbed on behind me and we headed for the dance in Newmarket. He used to call my motorbike 'the chicken chaser', but he never refused a lift to a dance.

He fed me one chip at a time like I was some sort of performing seal. When the chips were gone, Joey tried to light a cigarette but he couldn't get the Bic lighter to flame. I don't think he realised he was on the back of a motorbike. I think he imagined that he was on a train or something. He must have lost a dozen cigarettes along the road to Newmarket.

The moon lit up the road better than the fuzzy headlight on the motorbike. Even though I never got it beyond fifty miles an hour, the trees and ditches sped past us like we were in a film. Driving through Dromina, Joey shouted at me to stop. He threatened to jump off if I didn't. So we stopped outside a bar called The Case is Altered.

When we entered the bar, everyone turned to look at us, like we'd disturbed something. The bar man sat on a cushion on top of a barrel of Smithwick's behind the counter. He looked a lot like Fat Andy did ten years ago. I called for a Bulmers for Joey and a Guinness for myself, on account of there being nothing like Guinness to wash the flies out of the throat. There must have been twenty people in the bar, and when they weren't watching *The Late Late Show* on the television, they were watching us.

Joey discussed with the barman the prospects of the Cork football team in the All-Ireland.

I drained my pint in six or seven gulps and thought about ordering another one but Joey wanted to head for the dance.

Outside on the street Joey took a long piss against

an ESB pole before getting back on the motorbike.

The sky was full with stars and the clatter of the engine woke farm dogs along the road to Newmarket. Joey barked back at the dogs. 'Ahooo,' he howled.

He held on tightly and recited what Frederic had said as though I hadn't been there in Fat Andy's myself. I could feel his body vibrate with laughter.

In Newmarket, I parked the bike in a ditch by the river. My hands were numb from the motorbike. The sounds of guitars and beating drums and unintelligible singing came rolling down the hill and I hurried towards the lights of the Hi-Land ballroom.

I stopped in the street to give my brogues a wipe of a handkerchief and I licked the palms of my hands and tried to dampen down my hair.

Then I realised Joey wasn't with me. I looked around but didn't see him anywhere. I tried to remember when I'd last seen him and I couldn't remember.

I pulled the motorbike out of the ditch and drove back down the road towards Dromina. The barman in The Case is Altered was still sitting on the barrel of Smithwick's but there was no sign of Joey.

In the moonlight I drove slowly towards Newmarket again and called out Joey's name. Images of

Fat Andy and the cattle dealer came to mind, as well as those of Frederic the South African and his colleagues, but I couldn't recall when I'd last spoken to Joey. I slowed to a crawl by every crossroads and called out his name.

The sun was coming up when I found Joey, face down in a ditch by a humpback bridge, halfway between Dromina and Newmarket. His face was a battered mess of blood and torn skin. I knelt beside him and held him in my arms.

To my eternal shame, I debated with myself whether I should leave him there and go home. There was nothing I could do for him now. No one would know we had been together, except maybe for that publican in Dromina.

Perhaps he'd fallen asleep and slipped off the back of the motorbike. Perhaps he'd jumped off. I don't know. I don't remember. Maybe we hit something on the road—I don't know. There wasn't a scratch on the Honda 50. So I don't know. I don't remember.

A car stopped. A woman in a head scarf got out. It was Nelly O'Rourke from the Main Street. From a distance she called to me. 'Are you alright?'

'It's my friend, Joey,' I said. 'He's dead.'

She blessed herself.

The back doors of her Cortina opened and two boys stepped out. The older boy had a mass of curls in his blonde hair and he brushed past his mother to get a better look at Joey. The younger boy was dark and wore short pants. He stood by his mother's side. His head cocked to the side as he caught hold of her hand.

Nine

Avenger

A story from the past

Player: Carl O'Shea

Avenger

When my mother ran off with a greaser from Duffy's circus, my father built a bonfire in our backyard. He piled up all her clothes, perfumes, books and Carpenters records, and soaked the lot with kerosene. He gripped the collar of my T-shirt and shoved a giant box of matches into my hands. He barked at me to strike a match. I wouldn't do it. He vowed to clatter the shit out of me if I didn't.

So I did.

The fire began with a *whump*. The clothes frizzled in the heat, the perfume bottles exploded and the vinyl melted. The smoke was black as tar. I wanted to go back inside the house but my father kept hold of me and made me watch. After that, I was not allowed to mention her name in his presence again.

My father told people my mother had ran off with a clown from the circus but he wasn't a clown: he was a greaser. And he was once my father's best friend.

The women who lived on our street brought pots of stew and beef pies for days after she left. My father didn't bother to clean or return any of their casserole dishes, so eventually they stopped feeding us.

When it was time for my confirmation, my father's

sister, Eileen, came to live with us for a while. To help me get 'prepared', she said. She and my father were always arguing about something or other: about the heating not being on, about the immersion not being on or about me.

And so it went.

Then my father decided to take another tour with the merchant navy. Eileen wanted to stay on in our house while he was gone, but my father insisted she go back to Dublin. He made me go live with Nana on Bishop Brown's Terrace. Nana is my mother's mother. Her house had that hospital smell. She gave me a room with a creaky bed and grey nylon curtains. It used to be my mother's room when she was a child.

Nana bought me a yellow BMX Chopper. It had a gear stick like a car and I taught myself how to do wheelies. Nana took me to Mass every Sunday and taught me prayers like the Our Father, and Hail, Holy Queen. She never got dinner at the chipper.

Six months later, my father returned from his tour. He brought home masks from Africa that were carved by cannibals. He moved back into our old house, but I stayed with Nana.

***

My girlfriend's name was Angie. She lived three houses

169

down from Nana's. Throughout school, it was always Angie and me. We recorded C60 music tapes for each other. When Angie made a tape, she would draw a portrait of the band on the cassette cover. She wanted to be a graphic designer; I wanted to be a roadie for a rock and roll band. I loved Angie more than anything. I loved her name—I loved the sound of it. I was always a big Stones fan.

When I finished school my father tried to get me to enlist in the merchant navy. The thought of being stuck with him, on some ship, in the middle of the ocean, was my idea of hell on earth.

Angie got a job as a cleaner in the meat factory in Ballyhea. I went on the dole with the rest of my mates. Angie and I got married when we both reached nineteen. We had our wedding reception in the GAA club. My best man was my school friend, Dixie O'Neill.

Nana wanted me to invite my mother. She didn't ever say this to me or Angie, but I know that's what she wanted.

At the reception, my father looked almost handsome in his blue tux. You couldn't imagine that his body was covered with tattoos—one for every tour of duty with the merchant navy. He welcomed Angie's relatives with handshakes and slaps on the back. During the meal he sat next to Angie's mother, Rosie. Nana sat at the other end of the table, next to Mick, Angie's father. It was my father who toasted the bridesmaids when it should have been my best man, Dixie.

Mick welcomed me into his family. Then me and Angie danced our first dance as a married couple to her favourite song, 'I Want To Know What Love Is' by Foreigner. After that, the wedding band played old-time waltzes for most of the night.

Later that evening my father took to the stage. He held the mic in one hand and a cigarette in the other. Some of the guests clapped and cheered him, like he was the one who just got married. My father scratched his head and pretended to have to think about what to sing; everyone knew what he was going to sing. There were more cheers from the wedding guests and then he crooned the opening words to 'Strangers in the Night'. Angie had to shush her aunts from chattering.

As always, my father sang too fast and the band couldn't keep up. He walked around the stage like he was Sinatra. Some of the wedding guests stood and clapped in time to the music. Everyone waited for him to get to the bit when they could join in with their 'dooby dooby do's'. Then, just before he came to the 'dooby dooby do's' my father stopped singing. The band played on. They finally caught up with him but he stepped down off the stage and walked across the dance floor to where one of Angie's uncles, Sticky Murphy, was sitting. My father bawled at Sticky for laughing during his rendition of 'Strangers in the Night'.

The band spluttered to a stop.

Sticky held his hands up in apology and my father punched Sticky in the nose. I rushed to pull my father away. He pushed me against the wall. Dixie came over and we managed to get my father outside to the ball alley of the GAA club. Dixie calmed him down while I went back inside and bought Sticky another pint.

Sticky turned to me and said, 'What did I do?'

The band struck up 'The Hucklebuck'. The dancefloor slowly filled again. Angie was in tears, surrounded by a wall of bridesmaids. Nana and me picked up the black-and-white photographs of GAA players that had been pulled off the walls during the commotion. I bought her another Winter's Tale.

Our honeymoon was a week in some dive B&B in Ballybunion. It never stopped raining the whole time. We didn't care.

We rented a flat above the Pound Shop on Main

Street in Rathluirc. Angie and me had trouble sharing space together. When I was living with Nana, we could live separate lives under the one roof. Nana pretty much stayed in the kitchen or her bedroom, and I came and went as I pleased. But living with Angie meant sharing a double bed and having to talk over the cornflakes. Angie was no cook and I've never been great at the tidying up. She said everywhere she looked there was a wet towel hanging off something.

And so it went.

When the Ambassador Hotel was built I got a job as a kitchen porter. It was good to work again. I ate all my meals in the hotel and slept on the couch in the sitting room back in the flat. When I finished work, I went straight to Dixie's place, Nana's or The Auld Triangle. Days would go by without me seeing Angie.

Nana wanted me to talk with Father Fergus, 'to unburden myself'. That phrase sounded awkward in her mouth—it was like she had swallowed too much food. When Nana got an idea into her head, she persisted with it like a dog with a bone.

'Tell him everything, absolutely everything,' she said. 'You're not the first man to have woman trouble, and you won't be the last. Whatever you have to say, he's heard

173

it all before.'

There wasn't going to be peace until I gave in. So I gave in.

Nana's Volkswagen struggled up the hill to the priest's bungalow. The gravel crunched beneath my Doc Martens. A brass porch light glowed warmly in the dark.

When I pressed the bell, a chime rang inside the house. Father Fergus answered with a shout on the second chime. He was holding a leather-bound book when he opened the door. It felt like I'd interrupted his prayers. He was young, in his thirties, but I'd been warned by Nana to call him 'Father'. He was clean-shaven and his face had that colour of someone who never sees the sun.

He led me to the sitting room, where a coal fire was blazing. A naked light bulb hung from the ceiling. The light was brighter than normal, like he was using a 100-watt bulb. The floral curtains were drawn. An antique-looking sideboard had bottles of every kind of spirit on display

We sat in armchairs on either side of the fire. We talked about Nana but, God love her, a discussion about Nana will always be brief. Soon we fell silent and both of us stared at the flames. The coal had been arranged in a neat pile. Father Fergus offered me a Mikado biscuit but I refused. He took two biscuits, placed one on top of the other like he was making a sandwich and popped it into his mouth. Then he popped in another two. He licked pink coconut flakes off the palms of his hands.

'What would you like to drink, Carl?'

'I'm okay, Father. I have the car outside, like.'

'Relax, relax. Don't be worried about that at all. We have important things to discuss. Have something.'

'Maybe a small Powers, if you have it?'

He poured two doubles into square crystal glasses. He gave me a linen coaster with the whiskey and we were back to discussing Nana again; he called her a 'dote'. Father Fergus became quiet again and pressed his fingers together like he was deep in prayer. I was dreading he'd launch into a decade of the Rosary. That would've been just the kind of thing that Nana would've wanted him to do.

The silence was only broken by some polite spitting of the coal fire. I took another sip of the Powers. Then I realised he was waiting for me to spill the goods. I took a breath and I began to 'unburden' myself. I told him about the troubles that Angie and me were having. Father Fergus knew Angie's parents from church but not Angie. He nodded his head like he'd heard plenty stories like this before. I began to feel more comfortable, talking about Angie and me. He joined his palms together like a child at

175

Holy Communion and he rested his head on his fingertips.

'When did you and Angela start having sexual relations?' he asked.

I nearly fell off the armchair. I thought about standing up and going home, but I didn't. I hesitated a long time before answering and I don't understand why I answered, but I did. He poured another double measure of Powers into my glass. He didn't ask if I wanted a top-up; he knew I did. I slid my armchair away from the heat of the fire.

I told him about my father. I told him about my mother. I could hear myself speak and it sounded like someone else was doing the talking. I couldn't be stopped. The room went quiet again. After a while I realised I hadn't spoken in some time. Father Fergus stared at the fire. The flames had died and only red embers remained. It was like he could see something in there. All I could see were the embers. I could see the glass in my hand but I couldn't feel it anymore.

When I woke, I woke screaming. I wailed my lungs out in one long animal howl. I was drowning. I was drowning and screaming at the same time. I was on a carpet. Somebody's carpet. I was lying on my stomach on somebody's carpet. Someone was pushing a pillow down over my head. I could hardly breathe. I couldn't feel my arms. I couldn't feel my legs. Someone stroked my hair. Someone whispered, 'My lovely boy, lie still, my lovely boy.'

My hands had no strength. My legs had no strength. I swallowed air and wailed again. He took the pillow away and kissed my neck and my face. He smelled of Old Spice.

'Please be still, my lovely boy,' he said.

He lay on the carpet beside me. I could not move. He pushed the pillow under my head and stroked my face with his fingers. Then he pulled me face towards his and forced his mouth to mine. His teeth crashed into my teeth. He arranged my limbs about like a mortician. He spooned into me and we lay there for what seemed like forever.

He opened his collar and his shirt buttons. He opened my belt buckle. I tried to twist away from him. Only my shoulders moved.

He punched me in the chest. 'Stop that now.'

He grabbed a clump of my hair, pulled my head back and slapped my face. 'Stop that, there's no need to be like that.'

I saw the fire tongs. My fingers twitched. I watched my hand stretch in slow motion towards the tongs as though it were moving through its own accord. He pulled my boxer shorts to my knees. I clutched the tongs. I twisted my body and lashed the side of his head with the tongs.

'Jesus Christ. Jesus Christ. Oh, you fucker, you'll pay for that,' he said. He fell to the side and tended to his face. 'Look what you've done to my ear!'

I managed to get up on my knees. My legs felt like they were made of jelly. He rushed at me and knocked me down again. He lay on the ground next to me and I headbutted him. He roared in pain. I tried to get up again but my legs wouldn't stay straight. I dragged my body along the carpet like a snail. The door handle was out of reach. I smacked my body against the door. Father Fergus came towards me. The door sprung open. In the hallway, I pulled myself upright, and found the latch on the front door. I stumbled into the darkness outside. Somehow I found my way to Nana's car and somehow I was able to lock the doors. And then I passed out.

The garda knocking on the window with the torch was smirking. He shone it into every corner of the car. 'Anybody else with you? Are you on your own? Anyone with you?'

'Please help me. There's just me.'

'Just yourself?' he said.

'Please, you must help me.'

'What are you doing here?' he said.

'I'm hurt, please help me, please help me.'

'Sure, sure,' he said.

'Help me.'

'Sure, we'll help you. Why don't you open the door?'

And I did.

He pulled me out of the car and I fell head first onto the gravel. He struck me over the head with the butt of the torch. Then he kicked me in the chest.

I don't know why, but I started shouting, 'Dad, Dad, Dad!' while the guard beat me. But Dad was aboard a ship somewhere on the Indian Ocean. The Garda beat me over the head until I passed out again.

Nana came to the police station the next morning. She touched the bruises on my face. I looked up at her and I began to cry.

'It's alright, Carl. It's all over now.'

Nana lay her arm across my shoulders. She opened her handbag and found a tissue. She spat on it and used it to clean my face.

'I didn't do nothin', Nana. It was the priest.'

Nana brought me to my feet. We walked past the

reception desk where Sergeant Flynn rummaged through a box of lost and found. He never looked up.

I followed her out to her car, dragging my legs like a cripple.

'They're saying you attacked Father Fergus, looking for drink,' she said.

'You know that's not true. Don't you, Nana?'

'What do I know? Sergeant Flynn said you were asleep in the car when they found you, drunk out of your mind,' she said.

'He spiked my drink, Nana. The priest gave me a Mickey Finn. Do you know what a Mickey Finn is?'

'What do I know about Mickey Finn?'

'It was him, Father Fergus, who attacked me; please believe me.'

'Father Fergus attacked you? You want me to believe that Father Fergus attacked you?'

'He's an out and out psycho.'

'Why would he do that?' she said.

'He tried to rape me, Nana; the priest tried to rape me.'

'I don't understand, Carl. Why would he do that?'

'Why would he do that?' I said softly.

'Come home now—we'll get Doctor Adrian to see

to those cuts,' she said.

'I don't want a doctor. I just want sleep.'

The water in the shower was cold but I didn't care. I took a fistful of Quix washing-up liquid and I scrubbed my body. The water found every cut and bruise. My head pounded like something inside was trying to break out. I thought I would collapse in the tub.

I could hear Nana outside the bathroom door waiting while I dried myself. She was always lurking outside the bathroom door when I went to the toilet.

She made tea and drop scones. We ate in the kitchen in silence. In my old bedroom I listened to the radio, smoking one cigarette after another, still expecting to wake up from the nightmare. Any minute now I'd wake up. Any minute now. Kevin Keegan smiled down from the poster over my bed. 'Any minute now, my son', Kevin Keegan seemed to say. Eventually, I drifted off.

I woke screaming, and kicking and punching the bedclothes. My body was covered in sweat. I got out of bed and paced around the bedroom. In the kitchen, I paced about the table. I couldn't stop; it was like I was rushing to get somewhere. It was dark outside. I'd slept for fourteen hours straight. Nana came into the kitchen. She made tea. Somehow it felt safe to go back to bed, now that she was awake.

Two days later, Nana and I went back to the garda station to file a complaint against Father Fergus. She wore her Sunday best clothes. We discovered that Father Fergus had already filed a complaint against me for breaking and entering, theft and assault.

'You've got this all arseways. I'm the one who was assaulted. *I'm* the victim. Don't you understand?'

There were two guards in the station. One wrote up my complaint, while the other pretended to be on a phone call. The one on the phone was the one who had whacked me over the head with the torch. I watched them give each other knowing looks. They thought they knew me. They didn't know me.

'I'm gonna beat the shit out of that priest,' I said.

'Listen to me, Carl,' said the garda writing the complaint. 'You go within an ass's roar of Father Fergus, and you'll be back in cell number one.'

'You don't understand. It was him. It was him! He gave me a Mickey Finn. I was out cold. He tried to rape me. Don't you understand? It was him.'

'That's what you say, Carl. That's what you say. Father Fergus says something different,' said the garda.

'Look, I never robbed him. I went to his house

182

because I was looking for his help. He invited me into his house, like.'

'Help with what?'

'Help. You know, help?'

'What kind of help does a fella need from a priest in the middle of the night?' he said.

'If you must know—marriage advice.'

The garda sniggered. The one on the phone stopped pretending to be on a call. I kicked the wall.

Nana pulled me away from the counter, holding my arm until we reached the street. She told me to wait while she went back inside the garda station. I lit up a Kent Light. I could feel the cuts in my mouth with my tongue. I walked around her car, kicking the tyres. Nana came back outside. We got into the car.

'Well?' I said.

She pulled onto the Main Street without checking the traffic from the right. A bread van came rushing down from the Limerick Road had to slam on the brakes. The driver blared the horn and gave Nana the two fingers. She drove on down the Main Street completely unaware. The car lurched along the street, past the Credit Union and The Greasy Spoon.

'Well?' I said again.

Nana took a deep breath.

'Father Fergus will probably not press charges against you, if you let it go now… It may be best.'

'My fucking ears don't believe what I'm hearing, Nana, Nana. Not you too. Please tell me, not you too.'

'I don't know what to think,' she said.

'For fuck's sake, Nana, it was you told me to meet the cunt.'

'Don't talk to me like that.' She held a palm up. 'Your father talks like that. Don't you ever talk to me like that.'

'I'm sorry, Nana, I'm sorry.'

'I don't know what happened, Carl; I wasn't there. You know what you're like after drink—you can be a holy show sometimes.'

'Oh no, Nana, sweet Jesus up in heaven, you have to believe me; I'm telling the truth.'

'The sergeant told me you're been fighting at the disco and you climbed the Daniel O'Connell statue again a couple of weeks ago and you fair promised me you'd never do that again,' she said.

'Look, Nana, Dixie met this girl and he told her what we used to get up to, as kids, I used to climb the Daniel O'Connell for a laugh, like, and so he bet me I wouldn't do it again.'

'So, you climbed the Daniel O'Connell in the middle of the night—and you pissed drunk—for a bet with gobsheen Dixie?'

'That's right, for the bet of a pint.'

'For the bet of a pint?' she said.

'That's right. Reached the top too.'

'How old are you, Carl?'

'We had a few pints and we were having a laugh, like.'

'You and that eejit Dixie are like the two oldest corner boys in Ireland. What about Angie? Have you any word from her?'

'No, Nana, we're not talking.'

'Maybe you should go and talk to her,' she said.

'Talk to Angie? I'm not talking to Angie. I won't do that.'

'Everybody says you attacked Father Fergus. Keep away from him; promise me that much,' she said.

***

When I entered The Auld Triangle, Fat Andy was behind the counter peeling his toenails. I took a stool at the counter by the television and ordered a pint of Carling. On the counter, the butt end of a Gitanes cigarette smouldered on the edge of a seashell ashtray. Fat Andy seemed puzzled by my order. Since my sixteenth birthday I'd been drinking pints of Carling in The Auld Triangle and now it was a problem.

'Pint of Carling, Andy,' I said again. Louder this time.

Fat Andy put his slippers back on. He looked around the bar like he was looking for permission from the others before he'd draw my pint. Dixie sat at the other end of the bar counter, by the darts board. He wore a Che Guevara tribute beard and a bleached denim jacket sawn off at the armpits. On the stool beside him, lay his green snooker case containing a screw-in billiards cue, like he was some sort of Rathluirc hitman. Next to Dixie was Foxy John. Next to Foxy John was Sticky Murphy. Then there were six or seven empty bar stools and me.

The Late Late Show was on the television. The sound was off. Kids in the TV studio were testing out Christmas toys. Space hoppers and skateboards.

Dixie glared at me. Sticky Murphy held his hands between his legs and giggled to himself. Foxy John, in his usual attire of snazzy Bond villain watched me through the Sweet Afton mirror behind the bar.

The turf fire was nearly out. Two pool ques lay

across the midget pool table. I lit a Kent Light and caught my own reflection in the mirror.

Sticky Murphy blew a load of snot onto the floor tiles. And for reasons only he would know, felt the need to say, 'excuse me'.

Dixie stood up to face the dartboard. He used his own darts—the ones with skull flights and spinning shafts. He stood on the chalk marked oche and drew the dart back and forth. The dart landed somewhere on the board with a soft thump and Dixie adjusted his stance and prepared to throw another one.

Fat Andy wobbled down to my end of the bar carrying the pint of Carling like it was something hot. He dialled up the volume on the television, and legged it back to the other end of the counter, just in case I might talk to him.

The kids on *The Late Late Show* spoke with posh Dublin accents. One of them even wore a red dicky bow. The Carling tasted cold and bitter. Dixie put his darts back in their case and wiped the scores on the chalkboard clean. I took another full gulp of my pint.

Foxy John and I exchanged more glances through the mirror. Dixie told them one of his stupid dirty jokes. Only Sticky laughed. Another gulp of my pint and, at last, only the froth remained. I delayed by the door a second too long. I heard one of them say, 'Fuck you, O'Shea.'

***

When Dad wrote that Nana wasn't well, I was living and working in a pub in Cricklewood, London called The Green Man. Nana wanted to see me again. There was no news in the letter and no enquiries as to my health or employment situation. Just the information that Nana hadn't seen me in years and wanted to see me again. I carried the letter around for days before ringing home.

'Hello?' I said.

'Hello? Who's this?' he said.

'It's me.'

'Who's this?' he said.

'It's me.'

'Oh, oh—it's you.'

'How is she?'

'She has pleurisy,' he said.

'She'll be alright, like?'

'No, she's not going to be alright,' he said and cleared his throat.

'I see.'

'She wants to see you,' he said.

'I know. You said in the letter.'

188

'I did, I did. Maybe you could phone later?'

'I have work later.'

'I see,' he said.

Nobody spoke for a while.

'You could get the ferry home,' he said. 'And then be back in London again in no time.'

'We'll see. I have to go now. I have to go to work.'

Nana died in November. I didn't go home for the funeral. Dad wrote me again. This time he included the death notice in *The Cork Examiner*. Dad didn't say if my mother turned up for the funeral, but I know now she didn't. Angie turned up for the funeral, crying her eyes out, like it was her own mother who'd died.

***

I worked there six days a week in The Green Man. I got a weekend off every month and the pay was good. The accommodation above the pub was free and most of the drinks were free. Teddy the owner, hired mostly Irish behind the counter. He used to say the Irish had a special understanding of alcohol. He was second-generation Irish himself.

In early December, Teddy told me that a new guy was starting work with me.

'Straight off the boat, this one. Gus is his name. Lovely lad—clean.'

When Teddy introduced me to Gus, I recognised him but he didn't recognise me. I couldn't believe it was him. He'd put on weight since we'd last met and he wore the casual clothes of a much younger man but it was him alright. His luggage was a single O'Neill's sports bag. He was the only Irish person I had ever met abroad who didn't enquire where I came from. Teddy gave him a room next to mine.

In my room I smoked a cigarette as I watched the traffic on the street below. Rain made the pedestrians run, and it made the cars and buses slower. I paced about my room. The sounds of the jukebox seeped up through the floorboards from the lounge below. The Wolfe Tones, again—'A Nation Once Again', again.

When Gus came down to work behind the bar, he smelled of aftershave. He was quick behind the counter and had a friendly way with customers. He didn't smoke but carried a box of matches in his waistcoat for anyone who needed a light.

Later that week I stood outside his bedroom door. Listening. I heard his bed creaking and I heard his moans. I took a swig out of a long-neck bottle of Bud. I knocked gently. I knocked again. He opened the door. His smile made me smile too. He stepped back for me to enter. Then I broke the bottle of Bud off his forehead. He fell to the floor, like a sack of potatoes. 'You don't remember me, do you, Father Fergus? I remember you, though. You fuck. I was one of your victims. Now you're one of mine.'

He curled up into a ball. His hands tried to cover his face.

'Well, Father Fergus, don't you remember me? Carl O'Shea from Rathluirc? Remember when you were the curate in Rathluirc? You were going to give me marital advice. What the fuck was I thinking about, asking a priest for marital advice? What the fuck was that about? You accused me of trying to rob drink from your house. You tried to rape me. You may as well have raped me.'

The neck of the bottle was still in my hand. The body of it jagged glass. Father Fergus offered no resistance. He began to cry.

'Do you remember me now, Father Fergus? Do you remember me? Carl O'Shea is my name.'

'I think I do. I don't know.'

'Were there many others like me? Were there ones who didn't get away? Ones who swallowed the Mickey Finn and whose shame kept them silent for ever more?'

191

'Please, don't. All I can say is I'm so sorry,' he said.

'Shut up, you cunt.'

I held the jagged glass to his throat. He looked like a little boy. 'Rainy Night in Soho' floated up from the jukebox. Time seemed to stand still. His mouth was ugly when he cried.

***

Teddy asked me what happened to Gus. He said he liked Gus. He said Gus was the most professional barman he'd ever hired. 'A pity,' he said, 'a real pity.'

The aul' fella was on the phone. He wanted me home for Nana's month's mind. He sounded different on the phone—resigned or something—I don't know what to call it. I asked about the chances of getting into the merchant navy. He perked up a bit and said it was a fine idea.

'Yes, indeed, a fine idea,' he said.

Ten

The Last Days of The Pavilion

A story from the past

Player: Burnt Toast

The Last Days of The Pavilion

My brother Dominic stands at the head of the cinema queue, in black drainpipe jeans and a Bruce Lee T-shirt. His hair is a hive of blond curls. He gives a sly wave to me; I'm hiding in the phone box across the street. I wave back. Dominic takes out a packet of cigarettes and lights up with his Zippo. He combs his hair into shape with a pocket comb.

Foxy John, the owner of The Pavilion, comes out to the street. He is small and round, like the Hitchcock cartoon outline. Mammy calls him the most dapper man in Rathluirc, with his tuxedo suits, crisp white shirts, red dicky bows and the shiniest shoes you've ever seen. Foxy John pulls Dixie O'Neill out of the queue and tells him to go home. Dixie is barred from The Pavilion for throwing bonbons over the balcony wall during the Easter revival of *The Ten Commandments*.

Foxy John talks to Dominic and glances over towards the phone box. I pick up the receiver and pretend I'm talking to my mother, even though I haven't put any money into the box and we don't even have a phone at home. I discover the phone handle is completely detached from the box. Someone has cut through the curly wire.

Probably Dixie O'Neill.

Dominic's girlfriend, Sarah, comes around the corner of Broad Street. Her hair is tied back in a ponytail and her dress is summer yellow. She carries a handbag on her wrist; it is tiny, like a doll's handbag. Sarah is pretty but not as pretty as her younger sister, Gina. Sarah is a junior hairdresser down at the Curl Up & Dye. She joins Dominic at the front of the queue. He puts his arm around her waist and gives her a peck on the cheek. Sarah blows kisses to me, like she's at the Cannes Film Festival.

Foxy John opens the cinema doors. Dominic gives me the thumbs-up sign. The queue empties into The Pavilion. I wait in the phone box. After a while, the cinema emergency exit gate opens a crack. I cross the road by the Christian Brothers monastery. Dominic pushes the gate open for me and I slip inside. We emerge into the darkness of the theatre balcony through gold-coloured velvet curtains that reek of rat piss. The balcony seats are the ones that Mammy calls 'the Gods'. Up on the screen there's an advertisement for Egan's sliced pans. Dominic and I recite the words of the corny voiceover. We find Sarah sitting in the back row.

When the light from the projector changes colours, you can see the faces in the crowd. Two rows below us is

Sticky Murphy, with his dirty grey suit and manky tie. He blows smoke rings up to the light; they grow ever larger before melting out of shape and sailing down towards the stalls on the ground floor.

The wall lights dim. Whistles break out around the cinema. A mineral bottle rattles its way down the steps towards the balcony wall. Dominic and Sarah sit face to face, their knees entwined. I can see Dominic's tongue darting in and out of her mouth. It's like he's some kind of frog and she's some kind of fly.

I get my Biro and my red Silvine notebook. I scribble down the title of the film—*A Room with a View*. The credits come rolling up. I scribble down the names of the cast, screenwriter and director.

Later, I turn to see what Dominic thinks of the film so far but he's not watching the screen. He's busy trying to open Sarah's blouse. She's busy pushing his hands away.

'Stop, Dom, stop,' Sarah says.

He stops and she presses her mouth to his again, like she's trying to eat him again.

I get out of my seat and steal down the steps to find a seat by the balcony wall. I make notes of some of the dialogue as the film unfolds. Sometimes, when I get lost in the story, I forget to take notes. It's always the bad films

I've the most written about.

When the lights come back on and the credits roll again, I rush up the steps to discuss the film with Dominic and Sarah, but they've already left. Sticky Murphy turns to me and laughs.

***

On Saturday morning, Mammy's in the kitchen scraping mud off Dominic's football boots with a kitchen knife. I'm eating porridge and burnt toast and listening to a play on the radio. Dominic's in bed reading his Harold Robbins book. Mammy puts the boots outside the back door to dry on top of yesterday's *Cork Examiner*. She makes three ham sandwiches; she puts two in the fridge for Dominic and me. She fills a plastic bag with a flask of tea, a couple of currant scones and a copy of *Time* magazine. She puts on her head scarf, kisses my forehead and heads off to catch the bus for the parochial pilgrimage to Knock Shrine.

It's pissing rain outside; there'll be no work on Dinny Canty's farm in Dromina for me today. Sitting by the kitchen table, I open my lever arch file of film reviews. Then I get Halliwell's *Film Guide* down off the bookshelf and start writing my review of *A Room with a View*.

Later, Dominic and Terry Leahy come into the

house from Doyle's pool hall. I hide my notebook in the bookshelf. Dominic opens the fridge and finds the ham sandwiches. He takes a bite out of one and slugs the milk straight from the bottle. I can feel them studying me. I say nothing.

'Not working today?' says Dominic.

'Naw, it's fair wet,' I say, without looking up from Halliwell's.

Terry rummages through the fridge. He takes a swig from the milk bottle.

'Tell you what, cove, I'll give you two crow bangers if you drive us to the dance tonight in Kilmallock,' says Dominic to me.

'What do I want with two crow bangers?'

'You could nail two rabbits with two crow bangers.' Terry takes a bite out of my sandwich.

'What the fuck do I want with two dead rabbits, cove?' I say.

'You could make a furry hat or something out of them,' says Terry.

'Don't you have hurling training tonight?' I ask.

'It's cancelled,' says Dominic. 'Now, will you do it or not?'

'I barely know how to drive,' I say.

198

'Sure you do. You know how to drive a tractor—same thing, like. For fuck's sake, if Mammy can do it, anyone can do it. I tell you what—I'll let you have the deck of cards with the naked ladies.'

'The ones Sticky Murphy sold you?'

'The very ones.'

'The ones you keep in the Henri Wintermans cigar box beneath the floorboards in your bedroom?'

'Yes.'

'I seen them cards already and, to be honest, I seen better, like. Why do you have to go to the dance in Kilmallock?'

'When you're older, I'll tell you all about Kilmallock girls. Make your head spin, cove,' says Dominic.

'Last time you were in Kilmallock, you got into a fight with the knackers,' I say.

'Naw, naw—this time we're only going for love, not aggravation, trust me,' Dominic holds his hands together as though in prayer.

'How will you get home after?' I say.

'We're not too worried about that,' says Terry. He pulls Dominic away from me and whispers something.

Dominic smiles broadly and turns his attention to

me. 'Tell you what, drive the car home from Kilmallock for us tonight, and I'll get Sarah to make a date for you with her sister, Gina. What do you think about that?'

'Really? Would you do that for me?'

'Why not?'

'Really? A date with Gina? You would do that for me? Jesus. Okay, I'll do it.'

Later in the evening, Dominic sits in the driver's seat of Mammy's green Ford Cortina. I'm in front and Terry's in the back. The car stinks of Hai Karate aftershave. Dominic pulls the statuette of Saint Joseph off the dashboard and sticks him in the glove compartment. 'Jesus doesn't need to know about any of this,' he says.

'You know it's not Jesus—it's Saint Joseph. Now put him back where he was,' I say.

'Listen up, cove: key, ignition, turn key, engine comes alive, see?' says Dominic. 'Wipers to get the rain off, see? Now check traffic behind, check in front, foot onto pedal here, move clutch into first gear and keep it in first gear until you get home. See, it's just the same as Dinny Canty's tractor. Clutch and brake, and never go beyond first gear, just like Mammy does. And don't forget to park the car right outside the house, exactly like Mammy has left it, or else she'll know.' He revs the engine good and loud, and pulls out onto the road.

'Now, the most important thing in a car is not the going: it's the stopping. It's important you remember that.'

Dominic turns the car around at Morrison's Mills and heads back down the Main Street. He gives a wave to everyone on the street he recognises, like he's the Pope of Rathluirc. He raises gravel and drain water outside the police station and we all laugh. He turns right down Chapel Street. I study the movement of his hands and his feet while he drives. He takes a pack of Marlboro out of his T-shirt sleeve. He gives the box a shake and miraculously one cigarette pops up out of the pack. He catches it with his mouth and throws the box back to Terry. Terry lights both of their cigarettes with Dominic's Zippo. The rain pelts down on the car.

A song from the 1970s blasts out of the speakers:
Mister, your eyes are full of hesitation …

Terry presses his face close to Dominic's, and the two of them sing the chorus together.

'*Yes sir, I can boogie, but I need a certain song*
I can boogie, boogie woogie, all night long …'

'God, those Baccara girls—man, oh man,' says Terry.

Dominic slows to a crawl. 'This is the most

dangerous part of the road. The humpback bridge up ahead. You have to go fair slow. Do you understand?'

'Sure.'

'Mammy always beeps the horn when she drives over this bridge. See the drop over there. Believe me, I'm driving to Kilmallock for years now and this bridge still gives me the willies.'

'I believe you.'

'Watch out for the muck savages. They're cutting silage now and there's tractors out every night,' says Terry.

'Slowly does it, alright—see, slowly,' says Dominic.

He parks the car by the Kilmallock GAA field. He gets out and pushes his seat forward so Terry can climb out. I slide over to the driver's seat. Terry spits on the footpath in a way that could only be seen as some sort of a challenge to the people of Kilmallock.

'Remember, first gear all the way home,' says Dominic.

'I remember, I remember.'

'You know which pedal is for go and which is for stop?'

'Of course I do. What about reverse?'

'You won't need reverse. Just point the car in the

direction home and shout giddy-up.'

'What will I tell Sarah if she calls around looking for you?'

'Tell her I'm at training with the hurling team.'

'Tell Sarah,' says Terry, 'that she and her friends should give a fella more than a peck on the cheek—tell her that they need to boogie, know what I mean? Boogie woogie, all night long.'

'Tell her I'll see her tomorrow. First gear, alright?' says Dominic.

'Alright.'

'Watch out for that bridge. Trust me, you'll be okay.'

'Okay.'

I scrape the gear stick into first and the Cortina flies across the road like it's Scalextric. I slam on the brake. My head slams against the steering wheel. The car shudders and dies. I turn the ignition and the car comes alive again. I push the clutch to the floorboards and ram the gear stick into first. The car jolts forward and I hold the steering in both hands.

'For fuck's sake, slow down!' Dominic shouts.

I wish I'd the nerve to take my hands off the wheel, wind down the window and give him the two-finger salute.

I pass the Jet petrol station and a couple of bungalows. I lift one hand off the steering wheel and try to find the radio without taking my eyes off the road. It takes a while to find Radio 2. Motoring along at 25 miles an hour. It's not so bad. Like Dominic says, 'Keep it in first all the way home and even if you do hit something, how bad can it be?'

A car comes behind me. The road is too narrow; it can't pass. The driver beeps the horn. The noise it makes sounds like Road Runner. He pulls the nose of his car right up to the boot of the Cortina. He slows back, letting me slide away and then he pulls right up again. I come to a straight stretch of road and now he has room to pass but he won't. He's going to teach me a lesson. A lorry comes towards me. I slow down to a crawl. The driver behind beeps his horn again.

I come to the bridge. I try to remember what Dominic said to me. The car stutters again and the engine dies. The Road Runner car behind nudges me. I get the engine started again. I steer it up the bridge, praying that I will not meet anything. The stone wall appears closer now and I can feel sweat in the small of my back, running down my Wranglers. A train comes tooting down the track. It goes *chucka-chucka* as it rushes beneath the bridge. I lose my grip on the steering wheel and let out a scream. Mammy's Cortina scrapes against the tiny mud verge by the stone wall. The car hops up and down, like a cripple trying to run, and somehow steers itself down the other side of the bridge. I take hold of the spinning steering wheel. The train whooshes by beneath me. I find first gear, and I'm back on the road again. The car behind me lets go another Road Runner beep before it turns off for Bruree.

I pass the church in Garrienderk, where the aul' fella used to take us for the quick Sunday Mass when he was alive. For a brief moment I consider taking my hands off the steering wheel to bless myself but I don't dare.

I park in front of our house on the Main Street, in roughly the same spot Mammy had left it. I slap the steering wheel. I could do this again.

***

I'm watching *The Late Late Show* when Mammy comes home from the pilgrimage. She has battered cod and chips in a plastic bag from The Greasy Spoon. I plate up the food. She folds the plastic bag and puts it in the drawer where she keeps the other plastic bags.

'And where's himself?' she asks.

'Off somewhere with Terry. The chips are cold.'

'Anything on *The Late Late*?'

'There was a fella on who can eat a pound of cheese in thirty seconds.'

'The cod is nice. How else was your day?' she asks.

'Same as yesterday. How was Knock?'

'Same as last time, and before you ask, the lame didn't arise and walk, and no one was cured of leprosy. Gay Byrne's after getting very old.'

'Did any of the deaf mutes start talking?'

'They didn't announce anything about that. So I can't say for definite. That was a lot of cheese to be eating in one go,' she said.

'It was.'

'Did they say what's the late film tonight?'

'It's a Hitchcock.'

'Great … I heard on the bus that Foxy John is closing the cinema,' she said.

'No, no, he can't do that. He can't do that.'

'He is. Some fella bought it for a supermarket. It's closing at the end of next month.'

'A supermarket? What the fuck do we want with a supermarket?'

'Stop the lights. I told you, I hate that kind of language. It's bad enough I have to listen to your brother. Let you be the first man in this family that speaks respectfully in this house.'

'I'm sorry, Mammy.'

'Put the kettle on. I have a Milky Bar in my bag for you.'

Later, stretched across my bed I try to finish a short story I have been writing in my little red Silvine notebook. The story is about a lonely troubled boy and his dog. The boy is younger than me and lives with his mother in Rathluirc. The father has died or has mysteriously run off; I haven't decided on which. The pages of the notebook are opened and blank and I have a Biro in my fist. I wait for the words to come.

I didn't know it then but it would take twenty years and more for me to finish this story. Meanwhile, all I can do is to scribble Gina's name in the notebook, over and over again.

My mother's copy of *The Long Valley* by John Steinbeck lies on top of my bedside locker. I want so much to grow up and go to the Salinas Valley in California and become a dirt farmer or maybe even a short story writer like Steinbeck, whichever, I don't mind.

It's almost dawn when Dominic knocks on my bedroom window. I let him in. He wants to talk about this Kilmallock girl he met. He tells me she has a job in the bank in Tralee and her own car. He'd told her his usual line about being a student doctor in Trinity College.

'I almost had her knickers off. Fuck I was *this* close. God, I'd have brought them home to show you. Then her fucking friend came along, looking to go home. Fuck sake.'

'Foxy John is closing the cinema.'

'I think her friend was pissed off 'cause Terry wouldn't shift her.'

'You're not listening. Foxy John's closing the cinema.'

'Yeah? That's a fucking tragedy. I'm going back to Kilmallock next Friday night. See if she's there again.'

'What about Sarah?'

'Well, if Sarah wants to join the Legion of Mary, she can. I'm going out with the Rose of Tralee.'

'Go to bed. You'll wake Mammy.'

***

Sunday night. I'm hiding in the phone box again. Dominic is at the front of the queue outside the cinema but this time he has Gina by his side. Gina gives a small wave to me. Foxy John opens the doors. I try to flatten my hair with spit. The collar of the shirt that Mammy ironed is cutting into my neck. I shine my shoes again with toilet paper. Twenty minutes later and there is no sign of Dominic. I cross the

208

road to the fire exit.

'Dominic, Dom? Are you there, Dominic?' I whisper. I give the galvanised gate a soft knock. 'Dom? Where are you?'

I hear a voice from the other side of the gate. 'Not tonight, son. Best you go home now,' says Foxy John.

I turn back towards the cinema door and I race up the stairs to the balcony. The cinema screen is showing an ad for engagement rings. Fellas wolf-whistle and make kissing sounds. I can't see Dominic and I can't see Gina. I see Sticky light up a cigarette. I turn to the screen as the censor's certificate rolls up. I stand there in the beam of light, my hair standing up outlined on the screen like I'm in the band with Echo and the Bunnymen.

I look around for Dominic and Gina. The light from the projector changes colour to bright white light and I can see faces clearly now. I see Dominic and Gina in the seats by the wall. I rush up the steps towards them. Dominic has an arm around her shoulder and his other hand is somewhere up her jumper. Sticky looks at me and his whole body is shaking with laughter. Gina's legs are stretched across Dominic's lap. He pulls her knickers down over her shoes and holds them up in triumph, for all to see—twirling them on his finger like some sort of international flag.

Eleven

'Go For Tuna'

2012

Player: Jerry Doyle

'Go For Tuna'

My bare back is drenched in sweat. The bed sheets are on the floor. I try to remember what I was dreaming about but I can never recall my dreams. I reach for the tobacco tin on the nightstand and light a rollie. I lie back and wonder why I can't get a decent night's sleep anymore. When I click play on the iPod, 'Nessun Dorma' comes blasting out of the Bose surround-sound speakers, like some Islamic call to prayer.

It's the June bank holiday Monday and it hasn't rained in two weeks. I don't know why they have bank holidays anymore—now that the country has gone bankrupt. Somebody should abolish them. People need to work every chance they get, not stand around a barbeque drinking beer while the economy flushes down the toilet. I have to close my café because of the holiday; I can't afford to pay my staff triple pay just because the banks are taking a break from fucking the country.

I can't afford to pay my staff, full stop.

Don't get me wrong: I'm all in favour of the common man; it's just I have a narrow definition of 'common man'.

I make some porridge and flick through *Buy & Sell*

212

magazine while I'm eating. I find I can't eat anymore without reading. In fact, I can't shit anymore without reading something either—but that's another story. When I was drinking, I never used to read. The hangovers made my eyes bleary and there's no point reading when you're drunk. But, nowadays, I read the way that I used to drink and I believe I've made up some lost ground over the years.

The Catering Equipment section is busy but there's nothing there I need for the café. Not anymore anyway. The back pages of the magazine are where they print the more interesting columns—the 'Love Lines'. Alas, no one wants a middle-aged man—generous of wit, girth and jowl—no one at all. Every woman nowadays wants a clean-shaven young buck for some 'good times'.

Placing an ad in the 'Men Looking for Women' column is a waste of time; you'll be lucky to get one response. And she'll be desperate. And you'll have to pretend you're looking for friendship or romance and not at all interested in sex. I don't want to fool anyone. I don't want to take advantage of anyone. There's nothing attractive about the vulnerable. So, I don't place ads anymore—I just respond to other people's ads if I find something interesting and appropriate.

And nobody wants to hear the truth from a man in

213

my position. Alas indeed, fate is against me, through health and virtue. I know the kind of response I'd get if I were to place an ad in the Lonely Hearts saying:

Middle-aged man with varicose veins.

Smokes forty rollies a day.

Needs to get laid.

Female heartbeat is only necessity.

I've a policy of never dismissing any woman who agrees to meet for a preliminary drink. There are some fellas that'll walk away if they don't like what they see on first inspection. I will always sit out an evening with any woman who has agreed to a date. I know I'm no George Clooney, and I don't expect to meet any Brigitte Bardots through the Miss Lonelyhearts columns. Some of the women I meet are very attractive and fresh-looking, and some are not so attractive and that's the way it goes. Some of them I can't wait to get into bed with, and some of them I wouldn't ride into battle.

A fella can expect the lady to shave a few years off her birth cert. A little excess weight on the hips is to be expected. A fella should dress smartly, bring flowers and should pay for the meal. Whenever I have a rendezvous, I always get my hair 'done' in Felix's in Cork city at least two days beforehand. That gives my hair time to 'settle'. The girls at Felix's are always saying that my hair is grand and thick.

Life must be simple for gay men. Relationships must be so uncomplicated. Between men there are so few mysteries. And if you're ever feeling lonesome? Go to a gay bar, and there'll always be someone willing to take you home. If you really need some company, as in right this minute, you can go to one of the more exotic joints and you won't even have to leave the bar.

The Main Street is deserted when I park the Jeep; even for a bank holiday it's eerily quiet. The sunshine makes me lazy and I stay in the car awhile listening to Gigli squeeze the life out of 'Turn and Surrender' on Lyric FM.

That's another thing with all this sunshine—it forces a fella to contend with the outdoors. I don't believe that the Irish were supposed to be an outdoor race of people. You can see this in the colour of our skin. It's not just white: it's milky white, and it burns easily and we have freckles just about everywhere. Everybody is talking about barbeques and the 'new going out' which is going out to your garden. It just doesn't seem natural to me. Gardens are for growing vegetables and parsley—which is what I do—and not for bloody barbeques.

In the café I turn off the alarm and open the windows in the toilets. Everything is always spic and span when Alice has been working the night before. Last night's takings are in the ground safe. Another quiet night. I complete the bank lodgement slip and fill the night deposit wallet.

There is an AA meeting at one o'clock in the Mercy Centre in Mallow and another in St Luke's Church on Patrick's Hill, in Cork city. The meeting in Cork has more Mallow people attending than the one in Mallow. This evening there's another meeting in St Clement's Hall in Limerick. That's me spoiled for choice. There are plenty of dating opportunities for a fella at the AA meetings. Lots of broken marriages, lots of lonely women. But that's not for me.

Looking out through the café window at the deserted street, I feel a short jolt of electricity pass through my chest. This is my body telling me the news. The news is that I have not yet taken my Seroxat. Sixty milligrams of this antidepressant per day keeps me safe from myself. It is the ultimate irony of prescription medicine addiction—

being addicted to a drug that makes you feel just like everybody else. The Seroxat doesn't give me a buzz, or a kick, or a rush—just the feelings of normality. The jolts of electricity move down my arms. They fizzle out somewhere in my fingertips. When the shivers abate I take the lodgement wallet, walk down to the bank and pop it down the night chute.

My date tonight calls herself Gloria. There have been plenty of Glorias. It's only when you've taken them out on several dates that they'll divulge their real names. Mostly my dates are widowed ladies looking for some last excitement before life runs out.

When I get home, I feed my two German shepherds—Emily and Laura—with scraps from the café. In the kitchen, I search through the ECCO shoebox that acts as my medicine cabinet but I can't find any Seroxat. I empty the contents of the shoebox onto the kitchen table. Tubes of Brolene and Deep Heat, packets of Panadol and Gaviscon, but there's no Seroxat. I keep an emergency tablet beneath my alarm clock on the bedside locker but when I look under the clock, I see that the emergency tablet is not the blue tube of Seroxat but a blue diamond of Viagra. That's another problem with bank holidays here—

no chemists open.

The bath fills with water. In my bedroom I play a CD on my Sony Boombox—*Rigoletto* with Maria Callas and Giuseppe di Stefano. This is a ritual before I venture out on a date. The CD player is wired to waterproof speakers in the bathroom. The volume drowns out the sound of water rushing from the taps. I undress and don a shower cap and try to read *The Examiner* while soaking in the tub. It's difficult to concentrate on any one article.

Gloria's personal ad had said she was looking for a 'soulmate', a 'non-drinker' and a 'non-smoker'. Well, that's me. I can be somebody's soulmate, I haven't had a drink in years and I can give up the cigarettes as soon as we start dating. Her phone message on the *Buy & Sell* contact service indicated a friendly, sophisticated woman of an indefinite age. The message I left for her was my attempt at something suave but sensitive.

After my bath, I rub Nivea moisturiser into my face and pat talcum powder into the nether regions. The Spanx smooths out my belly and there isn't a grey hair on my head. For first dates I always wear my black Louis Copeland jacket—the one with the silver lining and the thick pinstripes—and, of course, my Ralph Lauren chinos.

218

Then it's black leather shoes, white shirt, open at the collar with no tie. The effect I try to exude is of a successful man, but one who is unaware of his success, a well-travelled man of the world.

All the way to Mallow I chew Tic Tacs, trying to kill the smell of cigarettes. When I pass the closed-down cement factory outside Buttevant my favourite song, 'Go For Tuna', comes over the radio. I take this to be a good omen and tap out a beat on the steering wheel. I sing the lyrics in a low whisper. A bang on the bass drum and the choir chants wildly and I can hardly sit still anymore. I roll down the window and shout out the lyrics to the trees on the roadside.

'Go For Tuna.

Bring more tuna.

Send somebody for me please.

Send me blue cheese.

How thick are thieves ...'

I park on the street in front of the Plaza Hotel. There are six large-screen televisions in The Strong Man Bar. All are screening a golf tournament in Florida. No one in the bar is watching the golf. Sky's jingle music thumps from the TV sets and reverberates around the room like an audio boomerang. A baby cries. A bubble of nerves forms in my foot that makes my toes curl. The nerves tingle and slide up my leg, through my body and fizzle out somewhere in the back of my head. Drink can work as a short-term substitute for Seroxat but after just one taste of alcohol, there'd be no need for any kind of date.

I order a soda water with extra ice and a slice of lemon from a tiny Brazilian woman behind the bar. Her skin is the colour of French tobacco. She could be eighteen or fifty. She gives me the once-over. She's not impressed. In Ireland, the only guy in the bar with a drink problem is the guy drinking soda water.

She cuts a slice of lemon the size of a golf ball and stuffs it into a Slim Jim glass. In Mallow, extra ice means two cubes. I can't believe the price of soda water in this place. They're making more money out of a bottle of soda water than I'm making out of a mixed grill. The Brazilian could be pretty if she made an effort—she could do with a little waxing around the upper lip. I get the impression she's expecting a tip.

I check my hair in the mirror behind the counter and debate whether or not to give it another comb in the gents.

Gloria is probably here by now, somewhere, looking out for me. I hope she's not thin. Skinny women have too much bone and not enough pillow.

It amuses me when I hear women today talk about their sex drive being the equal of men's. Women are the equal of men in most things and the better of men in many, but a woman's appetite for sex is not the equal of a man's, or indeed anything near it. Poor old Tiger Woods is proof of this. His exploits are the fantasy of every man—who wouldn't want to be banging leggy cocktail waitresses from Hawaii to Havana? The doctors told Tiger he suffers from a 'sex addiction'. What man doesn't? If women have the sex drive of men, why aren't they arrested for kerb crawling?

The liquor bottles stacked on the shelves are the colours of balloons. The curious shapes and bizarre shades give the bar the look of a space-age sweet shop. Sometimes, when I can't sleep, I try to calculate how much money I've spent on drink over the years. I like to torture myself like this. I must've been continuously drunk from the age of seventeen until the age of twenty-seven. There have been a couple of brief relapses. Every few years, something happens and fate strikes me down.

Doubts get the better of me. I make a quick visit to the gents. Standing over the sink I brush my teeth with my finger and extract a stray hair protruding from each nostril. I conclude the girls at Felix's are indeed artists.

When I was young, I didn't think auld fellas like me thought about sex anymore. I assumed it was the kind of thing that'd fade away as a fella got older. If anything, the carnal thoughts are more frequent and more carnal, if that's possible. When I was drinking, I had little desire for sex. Company? Yes. Conversation? Definitely. But sex? No, not really. It's surprising to learn that I think about most other things in life much the same way that I have always thought about most things in life. I guess I had hoped that I'd be a little wiser by this stage.

Casually and with a most confident air, I stride through the airy hotel lobby, whistling 'Go For Tuna'. I slide up to the bar counter again and I'm satisfied with my reflection in the bar mirror. Discreetly I scan the bar: families eating burgers and chunky chips; a couple of yummy mummies sharing a tiramisu and a pair of suits drinking long-neck Coronas, playing mobile phone roulette.

There's a female sitting by the baby grand piano,

all dressed up and no one here to admire her but me. She's wearing a cream blouse, sunglasses and a navy pencil skirt. She's pretty—no, she is very pretty—too pretty. There's another female sitting on her own, engrossed in *The Irish Times*' crossword. Women who read *The Irish Times* tend not to place ads in the *Buy & Sell*. Besides, she's wearing one of those moss-green pants suits that women wear when sex is no longer on the menu.

By the street window an elderly couple share tea and Club Milks. One of them owns the Zimmer frame parked against the coffee table. Next to them is a youngish fella looking around the bar and busy writing into a notebook. Gloria is either late or has changed her mind about meeting me. That happens too. I could text her but I don't want to appear over anxious.

The ice in my soda water has completely melted.

If it comes to pass that Gloria does not turn up, there's plenty of time to make the meeting in St Luke's in Cork city. Purely for the sake of some sensual stimulation I swing back to check out the sex kitten sitting in the shadow of the baby grand one last time. She's truly delicious.

Fortune, like the moon, you are changeable indeed.

'Hello, I'm hoping that you might be Gloria?' I say.

'Yes and you must be Jerry with a *J*,' she says.

She stands up. We shake hands. I inhale her luxurious perfume. She's somewhere between forty-five and fifty years old but very well-preserved. Her skin is the colour of weak tea.

'Can I take a seat?'

'Of course, Jerry with a *J*, please, by all means.'

Her voice is soothing and full of veiled promise. I almost collapse onto the velvet armchair.

'May I buy you a drink, Gloria, or would you like some more coffee perhaps?' I can't believe how confident my voice sounds.

'Well, I'm after two cups already.'

'Am I late? I'm so sorry. I try to never be late for anything,' I say.

'Relax, Jerry, you're not late,' she says with a smile. She looks like she bathes in organic honey.

As I get up to order coffee, I lower my eyes and check out the shape of her blouse. Like every man, I'm enslaved to my own biological impulses. The Brazilian waitress has the situation all sized up. She gives me the big eye, making no effort to hide her smirk. I order coffee for two and scones with cream and jam. I have to say 'scones' three times before she understands what I'm trying to order. I can't believe the prices that hotels charge for coffee and scones. A fella could get a T-bone steak in my café for the same price of the scones in the Plaza Hotel. How can my café ever make any money when I have customers that order tea for two with four cups?

I swallow a fistful of Tic Tacs and get back to attending to Gloria. As soon as we complete the obligatory comments on the weather, there's an unbearable silence when I cross and uncross my legs and fail to summon something worth saying.

'May I ask you, Jerry, a question or two of a personal nature?' she purrs.

'Certainly.'

'Are you married, Jerry?'

'No, of course not.'

'You're sure you're not married?'

'Gloria, I think I'd know if I was married.'

'Well, it's just there are men out there … who, you

know, take advantage, pretending they're not married. You can't imagine the type of men that are out there.' She raises her sculptured eyebrows and shakes her head.

'Yes, of course, of course. I can imagine. No, I mean I can't imagine … What I mean is … I can't imagine the type of men out there.'

'You said you were a successful businessman—an entrepreneur, I believe, is how you described yourself?'

'Well, I own several catering emporiums. A man has to keep busy or he'll surely end up in trouble. I'm a man of means but by no means king of the road. Aha. You could say I'm modestly successful perhaps, but I've my own motor car and my teeth are all my own.'

'Are you currently in a relationship and if not, how long has it been since your last serious relationship?' she says solemnly.

'Well I'm a single man these days. I'm not in any kind of relationship—I guess I've been single a fair while.'

'How long?' She smiles ever so pleasantly.

'Let's see. Five or six years.'

'And?'

'Her name was Peggy and we were going steady

but that was so long ago, it hardly matters now, Gloria?'

'Did you live together?' she says.

'We had sex in each other's homes. I don't know if that counts?' I don't know where these words are coming from. The words come spilling so fast out of my mouth it's like there's some ventriloquist saying the words and I'm just the puppet with the hand up his arse.

'What happened to the relationship?' Gloria frowns like she's unimpressed with me or perhaps about to really concentrate on my answer.

'To tell the truth, I'm not sure what happened. As I said, we were going steady. We were both working. Everything seemed fine. Then, I guess the romance seemed to escape from us, like air out of a balloon, at least, that's what Peggy said happened.'

'I'm sorry to have to ask these questions but I've learned over the years that it pays to be more direct in matters of the heart. I hope you don't find offence?'

'God, no. You're right. You're so right, best to get certain things out in the open … before … you know … just before … I guess.'

Gloria nervously smiles. 'Have you ever had sexual

relations with a man?'

'No, Gloria, I have not … never knowingly, anyway.'

Gloria consults a mental checklist. 'Usually I might ask a potential beau further questions of a … hygienic nature … but you appear so smartly turned out … as I said, you've no idea of the kind of man that's out there.'

'I do, I do. I mean I don't. I don't.'

'I must say I find you … very … debonair.'

'Let me reassure you, Gloria, my hygiene is more than adequate. I've even been known to change my underwear once in a while.' The Spanx cuts into my waist.

'You interest me, Jerry with a *J*. You may now question me.' She leans back into her armchair.

Now I can smell coconut oil from her. Maybe it's her perfume or maybe its shampoo or maybe it's her soap but all together it smells like exotic promises.

'Go on, don't be shy,' she says with a bat of the eyes.

'Questions are not so necessary for me. My gut instincts tell me what to do. If I like what I see, then I go with that.'

'And do you like what you see, Jerry?'

'Very much, Gloria, very much. Pardon me for being so frank. I find that at this hour of my life, coyness fades to nothing. I simply don't have the time anymore.'

'Is Jerry your real name?'

'It is. Is Gloria your real name?'

'My name is Gloria, as fancy takes it. Do you do this often, Jerry—meeting mature ladies through the personal ads?' Her accent is Cork but not as pronounced Cork as mine.

'Well, throughout my life, true love has never been smooth. I don't mean to be indelicate but now I prefer a more direct approach. Besides, we don't have Joe Dolan anymore to show us the way around the dance floor.'

Referring to Joe Dolan doesn't impress her. She lowers her eyes, like I have just committed some dreadful faux pas. I've probably embarrassed her; she doesn't look like a typical Joe Dolan fan. A thunderbolt of electricity zaps through my head like an internal fire cracker. My mouth is parched. I feel faint. How fucking long does it take to defrost a couple of curranty scones? Gloria studies her hands. She has an array of colourful rings on display.

Fuck Joe Dolan! Never once did I get lucky at one of his dances.

I study my hands, in chime with her, but I have no rings to twiddle. The jingles for Sky News cause her to gaze towards the telly.

It's time to dig out my all-star ice-breaker. 'Do you like to dance, Gloria?'

'I love to dance, do you? I love to tango and waltz. I love a man who can dance,' she says.

'Isn't it a shame that there are no ballrooms anymore?'

'They want discos now with laser lights and music made by computers,' she says.

'And the lyrics, Gloria, have you tried listening to the lyrics?'

'What lyrics? There are no lyrics,' she says.

'The ones that rhyme "love" with "dove" and "true" with "you"?'

'Oh, those kinds of lyrics,' she says.

'Yeah.'

'You're a bit of a card, Jerry.'

'I am, I am.'

'There are tea-time dances in the Metropole Hotel in Cork every Sunday now. They're very popular,' she says.

'Is that right?'

Okay, learning how to ballroom dance along with giving up the cigarettes, is another thing on my bucket list.

Pins and needles sensations break out in my arms. If I could stand and shake my legs out, the pins and needles would probably go away but I can't do that here in front of Gloria. I can hear myself breathe again.

Then, as fate would have it, I turn in my chair, searching for the bloody waitress and that's when I crash against her silver tray. A jug of pouring cream spills onto my Ralph Lauren chinos. The cups and scones tumble down to the carpet. Steaming coffee pours over my shoes. I stand up. I can't help it—I shout at the waitress. I become like a devil. The damning words come flooding out of my mouth. The waitress keeps grip of the tray but starts crying. Everyone in the bar turns towards us. Gloria shuts her eyes tight, like she's a contestant on *Who Wants To Be A Millionaire?* concentrating on the big question: should she risk everything on a hunch, or should she go fifty-fifty, or is it time to phone a friend?

There is a half-pound of semi-whipped cream sitting on my chinos, and beneath it, a stain the shape of Africa. My toes are raw from the coffee. The waitress is bawling her eyes out, like I had murdered her entire family when all I did was shout a bit. I put my arm around her waist and utter the only words in Spanish that I know, '*Soy Capitán, Soy Capitán.*'

That damned Sky TV is flashing action-replay images of some golfing fool in a tartan suit making a putt. The jingle music zaps and zings around the bar through the six televisions. I'm towering over this tiny Brazilian waitress and I give her a bear hug. '*Soy Capitán, Soy Capitán.*'

Somebody's baby begins to wail again; I guess that's my fault too. Gloria wrings her hands together, like she's washing them under a tap. She stands up.

'She's Brazilian, you fool. She speaks Portuguese, not Spanish. Do you know any Portuguese, Jerry? I didn't think so. Stop touching her, for God's sake. Can't you see you're making things worse?'

'I'm not touching anyone.' I try to gather the cream off my trousers using a teaspoon. I dump the cream in Gloria's empty coffee cup. The waitress won't go away.

She stands in front of us, like there's something else I can do for her. Maybe she wants that tip. I'm all light-headed. I could pass out standing up. It's awfully hot.

The hotel manager appears beside me in a black suit, white shirt and black leather tie. He stands by my side like a malevolent ghost. Gloria bats her eyelashes at him. The manager's deodorant is not getting the job done. He looks at Gloria, he looks at the Brazilian waitress crying about her momma and then he looks at me. He sees the stain on my pants and makes the decision that I'm the bad guy.

'Please, you must go now. Without delay. Don't pay—just go.'

***

Standing by a lamppost and rolling a cigarette, I look up at the waning moon. And I guess the waning moon looks right back at me. I pace about the footpath. Maybe she'll come out onto the street, maybe not. Best to wait and see.

The electric zaps and the dizzy feeling won't go away: it's like I'm looking down on the world from a great height and I'm going to fall.

It's too late for the AA meeting in St Luke's but there's another one in St Vincent's Church in Cork that starts at 10 p.m. Although it's not my favourite meeting—too many guys telling each other phoney war stories from their drinking days—I guess it's better than being alone.

I don't want to go home. I don't want the night to end on this note. In the morning I have an appointment to meet my bank manager about the café's perilous financial situation. The thought of it makes me even more weary. Later in the day I'll have to tell both my chefs I have no more work for them. Maybe it'll work as a chipper, there's always a market for burgers and chips. But it's the bank manager who will have the final say. I'll try and offload the café furniture and equipment in the *Buy & Sell*.

It's a warm night, a good night for drinking cold beer. There must be plenty of pubs in Mallow that remember me from the old days. I was always good for a song and never had to be reminded when it was my shout at the counter. Pins and needles sensations zap through my chest like I've won the jackpot on a fruit machine. I close my eyes tightly and I feel like I'm about to fall. I wrap my arms around the lamp post and curse that Mallow moon above me.

Twelve

The Electric Monkey

2013

Player: Alice Woods

The Electric Monkey

The passengers go around like bees in the lounge of Shannon airport. The pilots go by in twos and threes, in smart uniforms and shiny shoes. I watch the pilots watching the young flight attendants go by in fours and fives. It's like a Clark Kent convention checking out a flock of flying waitresses in leprechaun uniforms.

Every time I pass through an airport I take a photograph of myself in one of the photo booths. It's just to mark the spot, like a diary entry. I want a memento of what I looked like at that particular time of my life. I got a heap of these photo strips at my mom's house in Buffalo. I got 'em from everywhere: Boston, Atlantic City, New York, Dublin and Shannon. Each time I take a photo, I fill the photo booth a little bit more.

Once I made the decision to move back to New York City, everything about the decision felt just right. While I wait for the photos to be processed, my mind wanders to the events of the last few days.

***

I was working the Sunday night graveyard shift in the café. A guy came in with his girlfriend. His hoodie covered his

236

face like a shroud. Rainwater dripped off his pleather jacket.

He wanted a chicken snack box with curry sauce and two caramel latte coffees. He couldn't believe we don't serve lattes.

'We got Red Rocket coffee,' I said.

'Is that instant?' he said.

'Well, it ain't slow hon.'

'I'm not drinking that shite. I want a caramel latte,' said Pleather Jacket in a mock genteel tone of voice.

'Tole you already, hon, we don't have caramel latte. The lady with the recipe just upped an' died on us.'

His eyes bounced around, like he'd spent the night smoking Scooby snacks.

'Jesus, you're a fuckin' Yank,' he said.

He appeared pleased with his deductive powers.

'That's right, Sherlock. I'm a native Buffalo gal. Now that will be eight fifty-five, without the coffees.'

Slowly he started to pull change from his chinos. Then he started on the pockets of his pleather jacket. He dropped the change in a pile on the counter. He looked up at me and smiled. He wanted me to count. Some coins fell to the ground.

'Dixie, I'm hungry,' said the girlfriend.

'Keep the fucking change, missus,' said Dixie.

There was no change.

'Cheers, buddy,' I said.

He took the snack box and schlepped back to the table where his girlfriend was waiting. When he opened the box steam rose between them. The girlfriend wore a gold-coloured jumpsuit, with enough cleavage on display to make a Bond girl blush. She couldn't have been anything more than eighteen. Pleather Jacket had to be fifty.

Suddenly, the electric monkey in the claw machine came alive, lights twinkled and a ukulele strummed. The monkey sang, *I'm the king of the swingers—whoa! —the jungle VIP*. The monkey wore a big, dumb smile. The steel claw slid out of its cage and zapped about. It swooped and feigned a grab at one of the stuffed toys. It missed. The lights went out again on the electric monkey. The claw returned to its base, empty-handed. It's always empty-handed.

There's a photograph tacked to the side of the cash

register. It was taken outside in the alley, last summer. There's Jerry the café owner and Carl the chef, and standing between them is me. We're linking arms. Jerry had been going for the Slim Whitman look back then— check shirt and drooping moustache. Carl's wearing surfer shorts and his admiral's cap. I look ten pounds lighter.

The Sugar Sugar Café was a restaurant back then: table service, real food and percolated Robert Roberts coffee. There were oilskin tablecloths, paper napkins and a menu that was printed on laminated paper. Now, there's only instant coffee and the menu is written on the wall. But worst of all—now we got the claw machine.

I dialled down the heat on the deep fat fryer and gave the counter a wipe with a dishcloth. I straightened my paper hat and popped a French fry. Jerry never made us wear paper hats.

Then a guy came in looking for a batter burger. Whenever I see this guy I know what he wants. It's always 'batter burger, chips and a coke.' It used to be he wanted 'burnt toast, crispy rasher and a coffee'. We don't have that kind of food anymore. That's progress I guess.

I had three more hours to kill before I could shut the café and go home.

Jerry used to say there's no dogs or cats around Rathluirc anymore, not since the Chinese takeaway came to town. He used to say you couldn't leave waste food out in the alley overnight, on account of the number of scavenging dogs. But not anymore. Jerry used to say that he knew for a fact that meal number seven in The Golden Pagoda on Chapel Street would have been more accurately named 'Lassie Chow Mein'.

I don't understand how people can eat things like batter burgers or chips with curry sauce and cheese. But over here, they do. I think I 'd rather eat a bowl of 'Lassie Chow Mein' than eat a batter burger with curried chips.

Anyway, Burnt Toast paid for his snack and left.

The front door dragged back and in stumbled three young women, wearing striped pyjamas and Ugg boots. Each of them had their hair gathered on top, all beehive and grungy-looking, like they're in the band with Amy Winehouse. They approached the counter cautiously, like the floor was slippery. The monkey came alive again. Lights winked and the claw came alive. The three girls cracked up with laughter.

The pyjama girls studied the menu on the wall. I dunked a fresh basket of fries; the fryer spitting up grease at me. The oil flooded up, like it was high tide. I shook the basket and everything settled down again. I popped another French fry.

Shrieks erupted. One of the pyjama girls screamed she was gonna rip the hair off the head of the Bond girl. They started to chick-wrestle. The Bond girl was thrown to the floor. Someone's beehive hairdo deflated like a burst balloon.

One screamed, 'What are you doing with Dixie? You fucking slag!'

The other screamed, 'Filthy cow!'

Mr Pleather Jacket sat still and watched the catfight like it was something not really happening in front of him, like he was watching some chick-boxing on MTV.

The other pyjama girls shouted encouragement to their friend: 'Slap that bitch!'

I went to get my mop, lifted the counter hatch and started to twirl the mop about, like it was a baton. I shouted at the pyjama girls, 'Out! Get out now, we're closing.'

'Fuckin' Yanks, over here, stealing our jobs.'

'Move it, sister. Go home!' I shouted. I prodded them with the shit end of the mop. They stumbled towards the door. I helped Bond girl get up.

'It's them bitches that done it,' she said to me and put her boobs back in place.

Mr Pleather Jacket wiped curry sauce off his face with a napkin. He got up from his seat, picked up the snack box and winked at me as he exited. He and Bond girl climbed into a white souped-up pimp mobile with go-faster stripes. Rap music blasted out of the car. I mopped up the spilled ketchup and fries.

A box of curry chicken smashed against the window. The curry sauce stuck to the glass, like shit to a blanket.

Outside in the alley, I sat my butt down on a stack of Hellman's buckets. I lit the stub of a Marlboro. I stared at my watch. It was only 11 p.m. The watch was a present from Jerry. Sometime back he bought dozens of them in Lidl. He's been giving them away since. The watch has an image of white swans floating on a lake as a backdrop. Jerry thought it was cute.

***

When I got home, I was too tired to shower and I was way too tired to phone Mom back in Buffalo. In the kitchen, I poured myself two fingers of Jim Beam and took my drink to bed, knowing I reeked of burnt oil, batter and curry sauce. I lit up a cigarette and listened to the rain outside.

***

The next day, my little boy Billy turned thirteen years old. We had a birthday party after school, just the two of us. We played dance moves on the Wii I got him. We ate popcorn and drank oceans of sodas. Billy didn't want a cake. He had wanted a skateboard. No way was I buying him a board. We settled on the Wii and a skater's helmet. Billy doesn't do 'settle' so good—he does ceasefires instead. He has his 'spells' and he's on medication for that.

Lemme tell you, I have my problems and I'm on meds too. Blood pressure and other stuff. It's med city in our house. I bet most homes are the same but people won't fess up to it. Sometimes the atmosphere in our house is like a hell-hole the devil himself couldn't live in. And sometimes Billy and I manage to get through the day without throwing any forks or knives at each other.

Billy took the skater's helmet to bed. He fell asleep clutching it. I tried to prise it from his grip, but he wouldn't let go. I lifted his fingers, one by one. He moaned rattily. So cute. I pulled the duvet down and tickled him softly in the stomach. He let go the helmet and I put it in his locker.

Mom phoned. She wanted to wish Billy a happy birthday; she never rings at the right time. She wants us to come back to Buffalo. I could hear the ice cubes swirling around her highball glass, all the way from Lake Erie. She bitched about Obama again. She feels let down by the empty rhetoric of the president. I don't know why she feels let down. It's not like she voted for him: she's a Reagan Democrat. I couldn't get her off the damn phone. Later, I fell asleep on the couch in the middle of some Jennifer Aniston romcom.

'Where is my fucking helmet? You stupid bitch, what did you do with my helmet?' Billy stood over me. He flailed his arms against my face. 'Stupid bitch—where is my goddamn helmet?'

'Stop! Stop it, Billy. Get off me.'

'You took it—you took it off me. Stupid bitch.' He smacked the side of face.

'Stop this, stop this.'

He slapped my nose.

'I don't care where your stupid helmet is at.' I pushed him away.

He grabbed my hair and pulled. I punched him in the chest. He fell back.

'Ah, you fucking hurt me,' he shouted.

'Get the fuck out of here, now!'

'I know you took it. Why did you take it, Mom?'

'I didn't take it, Billy. Fuck you. The helmet's in your fucking locker. Get to bed now. You can forget about that board. That's never gonna happen now. We're done with that'

Billy backed towards the door.

'Stupid fat bitch,' he said.

'Get out of here.'

There is no hiding anything in my bathroom. The light is too bright. The walls are too white. There's an unkindness about the mirror. The bathwater pours loudly. I turned the key in the door before stepping into the bath. My ear throbbed and the blood streaming from my nose dirtied the bathwater.

***

'*Doink, doink, doink!*' The alarm went off. It was 6.30 a.m. '*Doink, doink, doink doink!*' I lay on the bed, neither sleeping nor dreaming—but awake and thinking. '*Doink, doink, doink doink!*'

I knocked on Billy's door at 7 a.m. He wasn't there. He was in the bathroom, already dressed in his school uniform. I watched him brush his teeth.

'Hey, Mom, we better get a move on—we don't want to be late.'

I fixed us some scrambled eggs and coffee. Billy only wanted toast and SunnyD.

'Billy, about last night?'

'It's okay, Mom, I know that you didn't mean to take my helmet.'

'No, Billy, it's not okay. We need to talk about it.'

'Whatever suits you, Mom, you know that. But later, okay, Mom? We can't be late for school.'

'But you told the doctors this wouldn't happen again.'

'Why do you have to say that?' he said.

'You hit me, Billy. We agreed on this. We said no more hitting.'

'You never took my helmet before.'

At the school gates, Billy pulled me towards him and kissed me on the forehead. He held my face in his hands, like he was the parent. He ran into swarms of schoolchildren and I stood, staring at his trail. The other moms talked to each other on the sidewalk. I sat in my car and closed my eyes. And I started thinking. Billy's next appointment with Doctor O'Flaherty was scheduled for twelve months' time.

Back at home, I fell asleep on the sofa and missed *Oprah*. That's the story of my life—always a day late and a dollar short.

Later, Mom was on the phone. She missed Billy. She has no grandchildren to spoil. All her friends have grandchildren, but not her. She said that Billy is like some virtual child, like in *The Sims*. I'm wondering where she heard about *The Sims*. She started to sob. She wants a letter—a long letter—from Billy. Not an email, but a letter she can carry around in her pocketbook like a tissue. A letter she can show her friends in the neighbourhood.

'I don't know what you are doin' over there, Alice. Those people aren't going to look after you and Billy. They don't have the doctors for that.'

'Mom, Mom ...'

'I see it on Fox News all the time. People over there, dying in hospitals every day. It's like Saturday night in Baghdad, for Chrissakes,' she said.

'Mom, we're doin' okay.'

'Say the word and I'll FedEx the air tickets. Have you back in Buffalo in no time. You wouldn't have to pay me back until you get set up over here.'

'I know that, Mom, I know that.'

'You just have to say an' I'll do it,' she said.

'It's just that Billy has to have routine, Mom. That's the important thing. You know that.'

'I know, Alice, I know.'

'Really, Mom, here is the best place for him. He's doing real good at school. He has friends now. Billy needs things to be stable. He loves the countryside. They got fresh air over here.'

'We got air too, Alice,' she said.

'Billy's doing good, Mom.'

'If you say so.'

'Mom, I've something to tell you.'

'Child needs his family around him.'

248

'I found a lump. Do you hear me, Mom? I have a lump. The doctor sent me to the hospital for tests. They took a sample, Mom.'

'Lemme tell ya, Alice, I had tests done one time for epilepsy. Oh, I don't know, it was back in the eighties, might have been the nineties, oh wait, it was the eighties. I was working for St Vincent's in the Village. Goddamn nuns always on about charity and never paid the union rate. The epilepsy test was free for the hospital staff, even for the maintenance. The doctors, ya know what they done? They made me stay up all night and put electrodes onto my brain, thought I was a computer or something. Of course they found nothing. They couldn't find the plague during the Middle Ages.'

'You're right, Mom, you're right.'

'Damn right, I'm right,' she said.

'Sure, sure.'

'I'm not feeling so great, Alice. My chest pains have gotten worse the past month.'

'What do the doctors say?'

'Did ya hear what I said about doctors? Don't talk to me about doctors. I've had it up to here with doctors.

What do they know? Any word from Billy's deadbeat dad?'

'I have to go to work now, Mom.'

'I told ya, didn't I tell ya? But ya wouldn't listen, would ya? That's the problem right there. If you'd only listen to your mother.'

When it was time for me to go to work, I prepared the table for Billy. There were pizzas and oven fries in the icebox for him and sodas in the refrigerator. Any luck and he'd be asleep in bed when I got home later.

In Lidl, I bought enough bottled water and frozen pizza for the week. I bought a fifth of Jim Beam, a slab of Dutch Gold and Billy's favourite, frozen éclairs.

**

At four in the morning, sipping a glass of Jim Beam, thoughts can become clearer or muddier, and sometimes both at the same time. I realised things would be so much easier if something was to happen to Billy. If his situation was resolved somehow. If the doctors were to commit him to some kind of institution, then he would be safe all the time. Even thinking about it brought relief. I could visit and I could work and I would know Billy was safe. Or if I provoked a violent argument and hit him over the head with a frying pan, kept hitting him, maybe he'd understand the pain I feel every day. If he slipped away, he'd be spared so much in the future. I know for sure he'd never survive without me. There's no one else on God's earth who can keep him safe—only me. In the future, his spells will get worse and he'll drift further and further into the world inside his head and I'll never be able to reach him again.

***

Jerry came through for the plane tickets home. I never asked him for the money; he just gave it to me. I guess Jerry just knew it was time for me to go home. He was sober when he gave it to me; I wouldn't have taken it if he had been shit-faced. Jerry's lost all interest in everything, now that he's sold the café, and he's fallen off the wagon again.

When the photos come sliding out of the slot, I pick up the strip by the edge. I blow on it. In the first photo the damn curtain was open, so you can only see white blurs. In the second photo, I made the mistake of trying to smile and all you can see is my big, fat 'burnt-out waitress' smile. The third photo is a little better; I look less animated—less of an electric monkey, I guess. But the fourth one is kind of cute. Billy's face is pressed to mine. His fingers are pulling

251

at the sides of his mouth and my hands are trying to cover my overbite as I laugh.

Thirteen

Shiane's First Communion

2013

Player: Carl O'Shea

Shiane's First Communion

I have this recurring dream.

It's night. I'm sitting behind the wheel of my taxicab. The glass in the dashboard is smashed. The windows are rolled down. The cold air whips around the car and keeps the tip of my cigarette ablaze. There's no one else in the taxicab.

I'm on a motorway, doing one hundred and forty kilometres per hour and I don't know if I'm chasing somebody or if somebody's chasing me. The tail lights of the cars in front are red and yellow. The headlights of the cars behind follow me close. I slow down to eighty and then speed up and slow again. I change lanes letting the traffic behind me overtake.

I move to the inside lane stick my head out the window and vomit into the wind. The wind gives me some of it back. There's a lay-by ahead and I park and watch the traffic zoom by. Whoever was chasing me is gone. Whoever I was chasing is gone too. I can hear myself breathe.

Then I wake up.

I fall asleep once more, and soon the dream starts all over again.

And so it goes.

***

Stuttering John sits by the kitchen table. He's wearing sunglasses and a filthy candy-striped nightgown. He looks like a blind transvestite. His brown and white greyhound is stretched across his lap. The dog's nose is stuck inside a tin of Charlie's Chunky Bites.

'Mo-mo-mo-mornin',' he says.

'What fucking time is it?' I ask.

'D-do I look li-li-like a fa-fella that—'

'A fella that what?'

'A fella that would have a wa-watch?'

The dog can't shake the tin off his nose. He whines and tries to pull the tin off with his paws. Stuttering John laughs at the dog. I scrape some Nescafé off the bottom of the jar while I wait for the kettle to boil. I pour the hot water into the jar.

'There's no milk in the fridge,' I say.

'I-is that r-r-right?'

'Fucking right, that's right.'

'N-no m-m-milk a tall?'

'No, no milk a tall, a tall.' I slam the fridge shut and head for the jacks.

'B-b-before y-you go in there, y-you might check

255

th-th—'

'The what?'

'The sh-sh—'

'The shower?'

'The sh-sh-shit.'

'The shit? What shit?

'The sh-sh-shit paper si-situation.'

***

I park my taxicab next to the Daniel O'Connell monument and cross Main Street to the Chicken Shack. I take a seat by the window. Now I can see if there's anyone looking for a taxi. Hard to believe now that I used to chef here. That was when Jerry Doyle owned the place. It used to be called The Sugar Sugar Café back then. There was a waitress who worked here; Alice was her name, an American. She was something else. She's gone now—back to New York. Now it's a fast food takeaway, the kind that encourages you to take away the food, fast.

Foxy John steers his Zimmer frame past the Cash For Gold shop and shuffles towards the passenger door of my taxicab. He peers in through the windows, like maybe I'm hiding on the floor or something. He can keep looking. Last time I gave him a lift, he fell asleep in the back seat and I thought for sure he was dead. I had to open his tie and shirt buttons. Then I discovered he'd pissed himself all over the seat. When I got him home, I had to lift him into his kitchen and sit him down on an armchair. Needless to say, I never got that fare.

***

Dixie O'Neill shuffles down the Main Street like he's the king of the shit. He looks inside the taxicab just like Foxy John did. He takes out his mobile and soon my phone dances on the plastic counter. It's like Dixie himself is reaching out to make it move. A missed call text comes through. The phone starts buzzing again. That's the thing about Dixie—he never lets up.

Dixie looks across the road, sees me by the café window and smiles. He crosses the Main Street, daring the traffic not to halt for him.

'How's it going, cove?' he says.

'Dixie.'

'Any news?' he says.

'No news.'

'What's the story then? Your phone not working or what?' he says.

'I've a Holy Communion gig on today.'

'That's great, Carl, that's great.'

'There's nothing great about the taxi business,

Dixie.'

'Maybe you need to get into another line of work,' he says.

'Who ya tellin'?'

'Exactly, Carl, something more lucrative and less in the line of public service,' he says.

'Is that what they teach you at Harvard?' I try smiling but Dixie looks at me coldly.

'No, that's what they teach you at pharma school,' he says.

'That business sounds too dangerous for me.'

'Danger has its own rewards,' he says.

'Dixie, I don't ever want to see the inside of a jail again.'

'Who's talking about jail? There's nobody going to jail. Fuck jail, like. Nobody ever has to go to jail,' he says.

'I can't do it, Dixie.'

'Can't do it. Fuck sake like. That's not something a friend says to a friend,' he says.

'I can't. You do what you have to do, and I'll do what I have to do and we'll forget all about it.'

'Carl, Carl, Carl. We could make beautiful money together. What could be more friendly than that?' Dixie smiles.

'I'm not doing it. You go ahead with your business and leave me out of it. Get one of the other taxis. Talk to Paudie O'Callaghan again. I won't say a word to anyone. You know you can trust me. We go back a long way.'

'We go back a long way, that's why you're my boy, Carl. Can I get you another coffee?' he says.

'No, I'm fine.'

'Are you sure? 'Cause it's no problem.' Dixie makes a face like I've hurt his feelings.

'I'm fine.'

'The world has changed, Carl, but you haven't. Things is different now … They don't call them "queers" anymore—they're "gay" now, and they don't call us "pushers" anymore—have you noticed that? We're "dealers" now. Words change their meaning—I like that. That's progress. But you know what, Carl? I don't like the word "no".'

'You were the best man at my wedding and now you're threatening me?'

'You make threats to a woman, Carl. You give a man the facts. We're not lads anymore. Everything now is for real. Do the decent thing and take the money.'

'I may not be decent, but I know what decent is. I'll think about it alright?'

Dixie lifts my coffee cup off the counter and takes a sip. 'Do you really want to be drinking this instant shit for the rest of your life? Really?' He walks out the door.

***

There're no numbers on the houses in O'Malley Park. The mother of the Holy Communion girl had said she'd be looking out for me and, true to her word, she pulls back the curtains, sees me and waves. Ten minutes later she's back at the window, waving out at me again but this time she looks totally flustered.

Another five minutes pass and the front door opens. The mother comes out of the house, wearing what looks like a purple tent. She totters down the garden path. Her heels sound like a two-legged horse. Halfway down the path, she turns around and goes back inside the house. A child appears by the front door. She's wearing a long, white Holy Communion dress and a tiara in her hair. She has a little white purse in one hand and a prayer book chained to the other. She gathers up the hem of her dress as she walks towards me. The mother comes rushing out of the house again. She runs ahead of the child and opens the side door of the taxi.

'How're ya, love?' the mother says to me. She's out of breath.

'I'm good. I'm good. How are you?'

''Tis hectic here this morning.'

She lays pages of *The Sun* across the back seats and places a Liverpool FC towel on top of the newspaper. She hoists the child onto the towel and flattens down the Communion dress.

'Don't move from that spot till I get your father out. I'll be right back.' She gives the child a tall white candle to hold.

The child opens and closes her little white purse. 'We're going to be late,' she says to me.

'What time is the Mass at?'

'It's at eleven, but Miss Burns wants us there at quarter past ten at the latest. The very latest. The very, very latest, she said. There's to be no messin'.'

'I see.'

'Mam's never on time.'

'I see.'

'No, you don't see, you don't see at all,' she says.

'Okay.'

'What's your name?' she says.

'My name is Carl.'

'That's the name of a girl. Oh my God, you have a girl's name—Carol!'

'I suppose I do. It's spelled different, though. What's your name?'

'My name is Shiane.'

'Lovely name.'

'Why did your mammy call you a girl's name?' she says.

'I guess at the time she thought it was sophisticated.'

'Is it?' she says.

'No, not a bit sophisticated.'

'My friend's name is Carol, Carol O'Rourke. Do you know her?' she says.

'No, I don't know her. And anyway, her name's probably spelled differently, besides, isn't Shiane the name of an Indian?'

'No it's not. Mammy says it's a beautiful name she saw on the telly.'

'I'm sorry, your mammy's right: it's a real beautiful name.'

'Mammy must hurry or he'll get mad again. Then there'll be trouble and we don't want any trouble so we don't, not today we don't. If we're late, Miss Burns will make more trouble.'

I twist the rear-view mirror to get a better look at

her. She stares right up at me, holding my gaze.

'Today is the most important day of my life. Today will be a special day. It will, please God. Today, I will receive Jesus Christ into my body for the very first time.'

'I guess.'

'The Holy Communion is one of the seven sacraments that a body can receive in their whole lives. Did you know that?'

'Is that right?'

'That's right, there's only seven,' she says.

'Seems a lot to me, I didn't know there was that many,' I say.

'Do you know what the last sacrament is?' she says.

'Is it marriage? Is marriage considered a sacrament these days?'

'No, silly, marriage is not the last sacrament you receive.'

'It was for me.'

'The last sacrament is "extreme function". You get that one if you die.' She nods her head solemnly.

'Let's not get that one today.'

The father comes out of the house. His grey suit is wrinkled. His white shirt is open to his gut. His hair is dark and slicked back, but the hair on his chest is white. He gives a wave to me as he paces about on the footpath, smoking.

'Is that—?'

'Yeah, that's Dad.'

The dad sits in front next to me. 'How're you doin', cove? How's the craic?' he says.

'How're things?' I say.

The mother comes out and sits in the back next to Shiane on top of the towel.

'I'll need a receipt for the Social Welfare when we're all done. That okay, love?' the mother says to me.

'That's fine.'

'Grandpa Larry's next, so,' says the mother. 'Turn right at the end of this road.'

The grandparents are already in the middle of the road in front of their house. They flag me down as wildly as they might flag down an ambulance bringing a defibrillator. Grandma has the sourest puss I've seen on another human being. She looks like one of those Pekingese dogs. They get in the back, sitting opposite Shiane and her mother. Grandma fusses over Shiane's dress.

'Can you get us as close to the church door as possible?' says the mother.

'Fuck sake, he'll do the best he can. Won't ya,

cove?' says the dad.

'I'll do the best I can.'

'Only asking, that's all,' says the mother.

'Give a man a chance,' says the dad.

We cut through the park and down by Smith's Road. Then it's back to the mayhem on the Main Street. There isn't a word out of the passengers. When I look into the mirror, Grandma stares back at me like I said something wrong. I park next to the galvanised statue of Charleen the Cow. The mother applies some lipstick.

'Is that a dog hair on your dress? For fuck's sake, there're dog hairs all over the taxi,' says the mother.

'For fuck's sake, will you look at them hairs?' says the grandma.

They stand by the roadside pulling dog hairs off Shiane's dress. I say nothing. I curse Stuttering John and his bastard greyhound.

The dad gets out and lights up a John Player Blue. He offers me a cigarette and I take it. Grandpa lights up his own cigarette, an unfiltered Player's.

'Nice weather,' I say.

'Great fucking weather altogether,' the dad says.

'What's that you say?' says Grandpa.

'Grand day today,' I say.

'Great fucking day altogether,' says Grandpa.

'We'll see you, so, in about an hour and a half?' says the mother to me. 'Will you try and park as close to the church as possible, will ya? It's my mam—she has awful arthritis.'

'That's no problem.'

'And what are you going to do about the fucking dog hairs?' she says.

'I'll give it another hoover,' I say.

'D'you know what you'll do now?' says the dad.

'What's that?' I say.

'Have your lunch in the hotel and charge it up to us. The Welfare will pick up the tab anyway.'

'I can't. I've customers waiting to be picked up. Thanks all the same.'

Cars pull up outside the church and deposit little angels on the footpath. It's like a congregation of midget princesses. The mothers wear expensive-looking hats, as though it's a dry run for being the mother of the bride. The travellers hang about at the church door. The women travellers wear gold-coloured clothes that are four sizes too small, and the men have their hair slicked back with Brylcreem.

I park by the O'Connell monument and read *The*

Examiner. The town seems busy but I don't get a fare. When I head back to the church, Shiane's dad knocks on the window and offers me a cigarette.

'Turning out to be a great day,' I say.

'Great fucking weather altogether,' he says.

'How did it go inside?'

'Grand, grand, but too fucking long. Jesus Christ, the bishop could have wrapped it up in twenty minutes if he cut out the boring bits. Be sure to give yourself a good big tip when you're all done with us, so, like,' he says.

'That's okay.'

'What's the best tip you ever got?'

'I don't know.'

'For fuck's sake, you must know,' he says.

'A bookie I took to Mallow racecourse one time gave me a tip of fifty euro.'

'How about a twenty spot for today? Add it onto the bill—the Welfare will cover it.'

He gets a coughing fit in the front seat of the taxi. Grandpa gets a coughing fit in the back of the taxi.

The mother talks to other mothers by the fountain. Grandma stands alone by the church steps and starts to shiver. Shiane emerges from the church, leading a bunch of her friends. They gather the hems of each other's dresses and run in formation, like wild geese, onto the grass lawn by the priest's house and down the road towards us.

'They'd want to hurry up,' says the grandpa.

'We'll get no fucking grub,' says the dad.

I turn the radio on. The others climb in. Shiane puts folded twenty-euro notes into her purse.

'I received the body of Christ in the form of Holy Communion,' she says, beaming at me in the mirror.

**

Stuttering John's still wearing his bathrobe and he's glued to Jeremy Kyle on the TV.

'Thi-this is fu-fu-fucking great craic,' he says.

'Yeah?'

'Yeah, there's fa-fa-fair thick cu-cu-cunts on the telly.'

He stretches across the couch and eats from a can of Ambrosia rice with a fork. The couch has been dragged across the room so that it's within touching distance of the TV set. Stuttering John won't use the TV remote, for fear of catching testicular cancer. He won't use a mobile phone for the same reason.

'Did you get milk?' I ask.

'I-I-I thought yo-you … I-I thought … I-I thought you w-w-were—'

'Forget it.'

'Okay, I will.'

'Did the landlord call?' I ask.

'He … he … he did, he did.'

'And? What did he say?'

'He … he … he said tha-that if we don't, if we don't pa-pa-pay the fu-fu-fu-fu …'

'Phone?'

'No … no … no he said that if we don't pa-pa-pay the fu-fu-fu- …'

'Fuel?'

'No … no … no he said that if we don't pa-pa-pay the fu-fu-fucking rent soon, we're o-o-out on the street.'

My phone rings. Dixie. He wants me to deliver a parcel of speed to some dopehead in Mitchelstown on Friday night.

'It's not heroin, like. For fuck's sake, Carl, it's only a bit of speed. We're not scumbags. No one's gonna die, like.'

'I said I'd think about it.'

'Well?'

'I'm thinking about it.'

'Good man—I'll fix you up Friday night?' he says.

'I said I'll think about it.'

Raindrops the size of frozen peas bounce off the window of the Chicken Shack. The chips are cold and the coffee tastes like warm puke. There's a claw machine by the wall, that comes alive every five minutes and plays some song from The Jungle Book and every time it happens I make a little jump out of my seat. There's a guy sitting by the door, who's busy writing in a little red notebook, but I get the feeling he's amused every time I get startled.

Across the street, five Holy Communion girls come out of The Auld Triangle—among them is Shiane. One of them has a dainty little umbrella but it's no protection against the rain. The others huddle together under a raincoat. The traffic stops to let them cross the street. The cars' headlights shine on the white sequins on their Communion dresses. The girls splash their way across and enter the Chicken Shack.

They sing a pop song about sharing an umbrella.

Shiane emerges from under the coat. She takes money out of her silk purse to pay for chips. The girls take their trays to a table. Their shoes are like ballet dancers' slippers.

'*Jaysus, Tommy, will you slow down!*' says one of the girls, taking off some cartoon characters from Sminky

Shorts.

'*Christ, he's clane lifting*,' says another.

'*Tommy's stone mad*,' says Shiane.

They laugh at their impressions.

'Heerrrrrreeee's Dixie,' he shouts, as he opens the café door. Rain drips off his jacket. He's grinning from ear to ear.

I bury my face in my James Lee Burke novel. Dixie approaches the Polish guy behind the counter, but can't seem to find the words to make an order. Instead, he starts laughing uncontrollably to some private joke only he heard. The Polish guy behind the counter straightens his paper hat and tries to summon a smile.

'How're ye girls?' says Dixie.

The Communion girls look up at him.

'Aren't ye gorgeous today?

'Leave us alone,' says Shiane.

'Will ye gimme a chip?' says Dixie laughing.

He vomits onto the floor. It's a yellow puddle. 'Better out than in,' he says, wiping his mouth. 'Hi, Polski, Polski. There's a mess over here that needs your attention—ha, ha, ha! How're the girls, anyway? Did ye see that girls? That's man-size, that is. Would any of ye help old Dixie find his way home?'

He sits down next to Shiane. He helps himself to some of her chips.

'Well, if it isn't Carl, my apprentice?' Dixie sees me.

I close the book and stand up. 'Come on, girls, I'll take ye back across the road. It's getting late now. Take your chips with you. We'll find your parents.'

'Okay, Carl,' says Shiane.

'Carl, my aul' pal, my aul' pal Carl. What's the story like?' Dixie's words fall slowly from his mouth. His arms are folded and he's almost horizontal in his seat.

The Holy Communion girls gather their chips and quickly slide out of their seats.

The rain has stopped. We cross the road to The Auld Triangle and I tell Shiane to let her parents know the taxicab's outside waiting to take them home.

Shiane leads her mother by the hand out of the pub. I get out of the taxicab and put my arm around the mother. She weighs a tonne.

'What about your dad?' I say.

'Dad's still talking to his friends. He's busy now but he'll be home in a minute.'

The mother falls face down on the floor of the cab. The cab groans like it's in pain. Shiane gets in, kneels next to her mother and strokes her hair. I get in the other side and pull the mother onto a seat.

'She's tired tonight,' the little girl says.

'It's been a long day,' I say.

I drive down the Main Street, taking a right by Charleen the Cow and passing the high stone walls of the School Yard theatre.

Shiane sings to her mother. It's the same song she sang earlier with her friends in the chipper but this time it's almost a whisper.

She searches through her mother's handbag for the keys to the house. Shiane turns on the lights in the hallway and the sitting room.

I walk the mother inside and put her down on the armchair.

'You'll be alright now, Mammy, you'll be grand now,' says Shiane as she pulls the curtains closed.

The mother moans.

'I've no money for you,' says Shiane.

'Don't worry about that. I guess your dad will be back soon too. Will you be okay?'

'I'll be fine here now, with Mammy to mind me.'

***

When I get back to the taxi rank, Dixie has left the Chicken

Shack. Some parents with their Communion girls flag the taxi to pull over but I keep going. I kill the taxi light.

I catch sight of Dixie walking down the Main Street by the billiards club. He's peering in through the cracked window. It starts to rain again. Dixie tries to run, but you can't outrun the rain. I follow him down Broad Street, where he stops for a long piss against the door of the public toilets. He stumbles down to the end of the street where he takes a left and crosses the road by the old Pavilion cinema. Then he takes a right by the fire station and walks on down the Kilmallock road to where the street lights don't work and the footpath runs out.

The wipers in the taxi beat a steady rhythm and push the rain aside. Dixie pulls his jacket over his head and becomes a moving shadow. He turns back to face my lights, sticking his thumb out, trying to hitch a lift.

I slow to a crawl. I dazzle him with the full headlights. I slow to a stop and gun the engine.

He turns and runs.

Maybe I should never have come back to this town. Who knows where I'd be now? Who knows what I'd be doing. Instead, I'm here, driving my taxicab. And there is Dixie, my old friend, hurtling towards another shadow.

Maybe it's time for me to sling my hook again.

Begin another life. Somewhere new.

I used to be a sailor once, with the merchant navy. That life ended in the rain too, somewhere in Panama, many years ago.

Fourteen

Yoghurt

Autumn 2013

Player: Burnt Toast

Yoghurt

The bus is chock-a-block with old ladies. Some are on their way to Mallow to visit relatives in the County Hospital and some for shopping and some for both. They chatter about the weather and their aches and pains while the bus trundles down the Main Street. We pass The Chicken Shack and the Sami Swoi. We pass the Post Office and the pebble dash house where I used to live with my mother and my brother Dominic.

I sit by the aisle, towards the back, next to an eccentric looking old lady in a black hat and Amish frock. She looks like Nanny Mcphee's mother.

I take out my Silvine notebook and open a fresh page. I'm trying to write a review for my film Blog. As usual my film reviews are more about going to the cinema than the film itself. This is a style I never set out to adapt, it just sort of evolved. Like becoming a blogger, sort of evolved. Like everything else in my life, it sort of evolved.

The bus stops in Buttevant outside a butcher's shop. The engine idles, the seats vibrate. Nobody gets on or off. It's like waiting on a stage coach in some Sergio Leone cowboy film. All we're short is tumbleweed and sunshine.

It starts to rain. It starts soft and soon turns into a

277

dark heavy kind of rain that pummels the widows and feels like it's going to last the whole day.

'Fuck it anyway,' says Nanny McPhee's mother.

The bus sets off again and a couple of kilometres outside Mallow, it pulls up by the boreen road to the County Hospital. As I alight I say thank you to the driver but he ignores me. It's like he's used up all the good graces allotted to this day's work on the old ladies and he has none left for me.

The rain lets up while we cross the road.

The passengers form a slow moving but orderly chain as they amble up the hill and under the stone archway that holds up the train tracks above us. A stream of flood water flows over the road beneath my boots. We resemble pilgrims on the lower foothills of Croagh Patrick. In no time I'm short of breath. Nanny McPhee's mother smiles smugly at me as she overtakes me on the footpath.

St. Gobnait's geriatric unit is to the right of the laundry. I light up a Gitanes and finish it before I press against the glass entrance door of the geriatric unit. The door won't push open and I try to gain the attention of Jerry, the security guard, but he's busy chatting on his mobile phone. I take a ten-cent coin out of my pocket and use it to knock on the glass. Jerry buzzes me in.

The first stench that hits you when you enter St. Gobnait's is the smell of hand disinfectant. The second smell is urine. The third smell is shit.

Jerry stays on the phone and indicates with a nod of his head that the visitor's book is on the desk beside him. A radio, the size of an envelope, plays music from Classical FM.

I sign my name as visitor and my mother's name as resident. Mrs Nollaig O'Rourke is her name but everyone calls her Nelly. I scan the list of names to see if anyone has visited her since I was last here. No one. There's always some vague hope that my brother Dominic will have paid a visit. He never does.

Jerry leans forward in his chair. The dye in his hair is leaving stains on the collar of his white shirt. The person at the end of the line is doing all the talking. Jerry's doing all of the listening. He hasn't shaved in a couple of days and his fingers are deeply stained with nicotine.

He puts his hand over the mouthpiece and looks up at me. 'What's up?'

'I'm here to my mother, Mrs Nelly O'Rourke.'

'I know that,' he says. 'You're hardly here to see me, are you?'

'Of course not. I'm visiting my mother.'

'Well do it then.'

My footsteps squeak on the polished linoleum floor. In the windowless corridor, Paul Henry prints adorn the walls, watercolour paintings of thatched cottages on mountain sides and peasants digging for potatoes.

An old woman sits on the floor smiling up at me. Her hair is wild and grey and she clutches a one-legged Barbie doll to her chest. She's wearing a striped blue and white t-shirt, pyjamas pants and pink sneakers. She pulls at Barbie's hair with a silver backed brush and speaks in a little girl's voice. She lets me know why she is scolding Barbie - for sneaking off without her.

In the Common Room two old people, one plump and one skinny, sit together in front of a large flat television. They are the Laurel and Hardy of St. Gobnait's but without the comedy. Each time I see my mother she seems to have shrunk in her clothes. She is fading away like a photograph in the sun. The plump gentleman next to her is Mr Johnson. He has scattered patches of red hair sticking to his skull like cactus on a desert. His face is blotchy white and covered in freckles.

Each of them holds a pot of peach yoghurt in outstretched hands, like they're holding candles. They are engrossed in an ad on the TV for Mercury Motor Insurance.

I remove my donkey jacket and sit on a plastic chair.

'Mammy, Mammy, it's me,' I say.

She's wearing a green paisley pyjamas top, black slacks and red slippers. She points to the television, encouraging me to pay attention to the ads.

'It's me, Mammy. It's me, Mammy. I've brought you a packet of Fruit Pastilles. Your favourite.'

She ignores the sweets and smiles patiently at me. Then she turns her attention back to the TV. I push the sweets into her slacks pocket.

I take this week's copy of *Woman's Way* out of my jacket pocket and hold it on display like I was a salesman with a brochure. She ignores the magazine. I open some of the colour pages for her, but she has no interest.

'Okay, Mammy, what are we watching?'

I use a finger to wipe off a little yoghurt from her chin.

Mr Johnson is wearing matching pyjamas top and bottoms and has a tartan blanket on his lap. He rocks back and forth in his chair, breathing in loud rhythmic grunts, 'N'huh, n'huh, n'huh'. He sounds like he's getting it on with his missus. He has splashes of yoghurt on his forehead, on his nose and on his chin. In between the 'N'huh's' he manages to indicate to me that there's something worth watching on the TV. He does this by stabbing a finger in the general direction of the TV set. 'N'huh, n'huh, n'huh'

It's the Jeremy Kyle show. The sound is mute but there's no need for sound on Jeremy Kyle.

'Mammy, how're they treating you? Alright?'

She turns towards me and smiles like the most generous and wisest and understanding of benefactors. Her young visitor must learn to appreciate Jeremy Kyle a little more and not interrupt.

Mammy dunks a finger into the yoghurt pot, scrapes off a sliver and sticks it in her mouth.

'Where's your spoon, Mammy? Did you lose your spoon?'

I search the floor and the chair for a spoon. When I

can't find any, I try to take the yogurt pot from her. Mammy grips the pot tighter. I wrestle with her bony fingers. She lets go a little whimper. Then the pot bursts and yoghurt oozes out between our entwined fingers. Some yoghurt falls on her lap but most falls on the linoleum floor. She gives me a wounded look.

'Oh Jesus, Mammy, I'm sorry. It's my fault. My fault. I'm sorry. I'm so sorry.'

Mr Johnson stops rocking his chair. All those 'N'huh, n'huh, n'huh's' come to a sudden halt. He looks towards me and the foxy tufts of hair seem to stand to attention. His mouth opens wide in slow motion disbelief.

'I didn't mean it,' I say to him.

Mammy points at the crushed yoghurt pot. Her little frame rises and falls and she begins to weep. I stand and then I sit and I put an arm across her and pull her close.

'I'm okay. It's going to be okay. I promise you Mammy, it'll be okay.'

I pick up the shell of the yoghurt pot and go find a toilet. When I return with a roll of toilet paper Mammy welcomes me back with a new generous smile and invites me to sit and watch the Jeremy Kyle show with her.

I tear off a length of toilet paper and begin cleaning her face and her pyjamas top.

'Mammy, can you listen to me for a minute? I want to tell you about my new position. I got another promotion. They made me junior partner in Rattigan, Palmer and Hodge. Can you believe it? I have a secretary now and my own parking space. It's all going well. Very well. I'm very busy now, of course. A lot of responsibilities entailed in this position.'

I clean her cold fingers, one by one.

'Dominic says hello ...he's doing great too. He has two little boys now, Eddie and PJ. Your grandchildren. Do you remember them? Eddie and PJ? They're all doing great. They miss you, Mammy, the grandkids, they really miss you.'

Mammy turns towards Mr Johnson and reaches out and quickly steals his pot of peach yoghurt. Before I can stop her, she has a finger inside the pot and raises a large scoop and sticks it in her mouth.

Mr Johnson is slow to register the theft of his yoghurt. He looks at his empty hands, he looks at Mammy's full hands and slowly the astonishment becomes written on his face. He grunts again, but louder. 'N'huh, n'huh, n'huh'. He rocks back and forward in a faster rhythm. He raises the grunting volume; like he's really getting it on. When he rocks back, the front legs of the chair lift off the floor, when he rocks forward, he slams the legs down against the floor. He roars, 'hump, hump, hump.' Like some sailor who hasn't been home from sea in months. 'Hump, Hump, Hump.' His blanket falls to the floor. 'Hump, Hump, Hump.'

I look around for a nurse or a hospital porter. There is none to be found. Mammy is oblivious to all the grunting and rocking going on beside her. She calmly scoops out finger-full after finger-full, from the yoghurt pot. I try to pull the pot away from her. Mammy has a surprisingly strong grip and, of course, she has all those years of the Irish Mammy's righteous indignation in a store somewhere in the back of her head.

I can't understand why the nurses or the porters can't hear Mr Johnson rocking and grunting. If there was this volume of rocking and grunting in some flea hole Mexican bordello someone would come running. Why doesn't someone come running?

Once again, the pot bursts and yoghurt squelches out between our fingers and the pot flies up into the air and

285

then plops down onto the linoleum floor.

Mr Johnson pulls his chair to a halt like a jockey might stop a runaway horse. There's a horrible nauseating climaxing trail-off to the last 'Hump, hump, hump'.

The three of us stare at the up-turned yoghurt pot. I let go of Mammy's fingers. She looks defeated but even in defeat, she looks dignified.

I dump the second yoghurt pot in a bin in the toilet. When I return, I use the toilet paper to clean the hands and faces of both Mammy and Mr Johnson.

Mr Johnson holds his chin out as though he's expecting a shave. The grunting begins again but it's only a steady trot, 'n'huh, n'huh, n'huh', and the two of them renew their focus on the Kyle show.

Along comes a care assistant pushing a catering trolley. She's humming some country and western song and announces her arrival from a distance. 'Hi everybody. How's everybody doin' today?'

'Hi, Alice,' I say.

'Does anybody want tea or coffee? I got cookies too if anybody wants them?'

Mammy and Mr Johnson beam up at Alice like

children at an ice cream van.

Alice gives them each a Marietta and pours a half a cup of tea into a plastic container for Mr Johnson. He lifts his shoulder to guard his tea and biscuits from theft.

'How you doin', hon?' says Alice as she rests her ample rear on the chair next to mine.

'I'm fine.'

'Are you taking care of yourself?' she says.

'Yes I am.'

'How's your mom doin'? she says.

'She's alright I guess.'

'Lemme tell you, this job has me worn out. Everyday somebody phones in sick. Every day it's the same thing. Then I got to do double the work. They got me in the kitchen if a chef pulls a sickie, they got me on the floor if an assistant pulls a sickie. They got me washing bodies and making beds, yadda, yadda. Pretty soon they gonna have me performing operations.' She lets go a long sigh. 'You know Carl? Carl the porter?'

'I know Carl.'

'He hasn't come to work in three days. They make

me cover for him. I'm all morning lifting people in and out of their beds. Lemme tell you, some of them old guys still got a bit of life left in 'em, if you know what I mean.'

Alice rises from her chair and pushes the trolley back down the corridor.

I turn towards Mammy. 'I have something here for you. Look. It's a photograph I found amongst your things. See here? There's you and there's Dominic. It's the day of my Holy Communion. That's St. Oliver's church. Do you remember? I took that photo. Do you remember Mam?'

Mammy takes hold of the postcard size photograph.

'Your name is Nollaig. Nelly, they call you. You used to be a seamstress. You used to love the cinema and Sinatra. Remember? There were two children, Dominic and me. I'm here, Mammy, I'm here.'

Mammy tries to return the photograph but I will not accept it.

'See this good looking lady here? That's you. And see here? that's Dominic beside you. Can't you remember? Can't you remember any of it?'

Mammy indulges me by taking another look at the photograph. A smile slowly develops. 'Dom' she whispers.

'Dom'.

'Yes, yes.'

'Dom.'

'Remember he tore a hole in his pants that morning of the Holy Communion and you had to sow the pants and you got so angry? And we were late for the Bishop.'

Mammy acknowledges my babbling with another indulgent smile. I wipe my eyes with the sleeve of my jumper, even though I hold a roll of tissue paper in my hands.

I hold her hands in mine and squeezes them gently.

Mr Johnson stands up and wanders down the hall. A man on a slow mission.

I put the photograph away.

'I've got to go. The taxi is waiting outside for me. I hope you're proud of me, Mammy, and all the things I've accomplished. You used to say to me "look after the books son and the books will look after you". You were right all along. Things are going great now. They're just great.'

Mammy points a bony finger towards the TV, there's an ad for Red Rocket coffee. She seems to urge the strange young man to pay attention.

'I know, Mammy. I promise I'll be quiet.'

I stand and kiss her on the forehead. 'Soon, Mammy, I'll be back soon. I promise I won't let it be so long the next time.'

*****

CPSIA information can be obtained
at www.ICGtesting.com
Printed in the USA
LVHW091701030419
612842LV00004B/889/P